City Lights From the Upside Down

∞

City Lights From the Upside Down

Stories by Alex Z. Salinas

SAR Press
Austin

Library of Congress Cataloging-in-Publication Data
Names: Salinas, Alex Z. | Salinas, Alex Z. 6/23/1989–. City Lights From the Upside Down.
Title: City Lights From the Upside Down: Stories by Alex Z. Salinas.
Description: Trade paperback edition. | Austin: SAR Press/William O. Pate II, 2021.
Identifiers: LCCN 2021912466 | ISBN 9781736177976 (softcover) | ISBN 9781736177969 (ebook)
Subjects: BISAC: FICTION / Short stories (single author). FICTION / Hispanic & Latino. FICTION / City Life. FICTION / Family Life / Siblings.

Published by
SAR Press/William O. Pate II
an imprint of *San Antonio Review*
2028 E. Ben White Boulevard #240-5735
Austin, Texas 78741
United States of America

The publisher's father, William O. Pate, has converted former family farmland in southwest Alabama into new growth forest and enrolled it in the U.S. Department of Agriculture's Conservation Reserve Program in support of climate-change mitigation, covering at least a portion of the renewable resources required to produce print editions of this book.

Typeset using Caladea, a free modern, friendly serif font family, designed by Carolina Giovagnoli and Andrés Torresi for Huerta Tipográfica.

Cover design by William O. Pate II.

Always read free at sareview.org.

Contents

Warming Up

∞

The novelist Philip Roth said when a writer is born into a family, the family is ruined.

I thought this as I raced the shadow of a cloud on an empty road midafternoon.

By raced, I mean I attempted remaining within the shadow. Shaded. As in, my skin's pale and melanoma is killing my mother.

The Texas sun is savage, especially to light-skinned Hispanics.

Years ago, I wrote a short story about an alcoholic mother. My mother read it.

"The words are beautiful, but it's so sad," she said.

I'm not a bad omen. But I'm warming up to wrecking ball.

Places

∞

I wasn't ready for Mom to die.

My cellphone buzzed while I was in the newsroom. I didn't recognize the caller. Probably another goddamn cable salesperson, I thought. It took me switching to a new provider before the old one realized I existed. They wanted me back, but I was done with them like a crazy ex.

My cell buzzed again, same number. Jesus, I thought.

I had little patience for things these days like waiting in line, listening to people talk and dealing with cable. My breakup with Marcela had me on edge.

"Hello," I answered coldly, before I would tell them to fuck off.

"Hi, is this Mark Vasquez, the son of Cathy Vasquez?" the caller asked. His accent was thick, but his English was polished.

"What? My mom? Who's calling?" I said.

"I'm sorry, sir. I'm Dr. Dennis Bhatt from Baptist Medical Center. I apologize for calling you like this, but I have some bad news. Do you have a minute, Mr. Vasquez?"

Mom had been involved in a multivehicle accident on the highway during rush hour, Doc said. It happened on her way home from work. The driver, who witnesses said was swerving in and out of lanes, crashed his truck into the passenger side of Mom's Mazda. Both plowed into other vehicles before an explosive stop into a guardrail. The driver died on impact; Mom was in critical condition. She was on the operating table in the ER, fighting for life. Doc said the driver was most likely drunk.

Only assholes drive drunk at 5 p.m., I thought. Maybe it was Dad.

"Come to the hospital soon, if you're able. I wouldn't ask you if this wasn't urgent. We're doing everything we can to help your mother," Doc said.

. . .

There was nothing they could do.

A body endures only so much before giving up. Mom's was shattered. Her lungs were crushed, her brain had hemorrhaged. Oxygen flow stopped. She died just before I arrived.

I was her only family there. My litter brother, Sam, was in Minnesota. My aunt Lydia, Mom's only sibling, was a fundamental product of her generation—a hippie-leftover doing God knows what God knows where. The last we'd heard from her was from an old postcard, a beautifully written message professing she'd always be our second mother. I doubt she could be reached.

"Dude, is Mom okay? Are you over there now?" Sam immediately asked when I answered his call. I'd texted him driving over to the hospital.

It was weird hearing Sam worried. His voice was usually monotone, distant. He'd smoked his way through college. He reminded me of The Dude from *The Big Lebowski*, except without long hair. Sometimes I think Sam only finished college because I did; he didn't want the label of Underachieving Younger Bro, but he'd tell you he didn't care.

"She's gone, Sam," I said.

"Oh God," he said softly.

There was a pause. I heard him cry.

. . .

I wasn't in the room when it happened, but I imagined Mom's last breath sounded painful. I imagined it gasped out of her broken body and evaporated into the air with the antiseptics that filled the ER.

I imagined she would've looked at me right before she went.

When I finally saw her, she was unrecognizable. Her face was battered, swollen and green. Her long, dark hair was matted with dried blood. Chunks of her scalp were missing. Her arms and legs were covered with bruises and lacerations. Her final moments must have been torture.

I touched one of her hands. It felt cold and foreign, like refrigerated meat. She'd done a lot with those hands, like data entry at the credit union to barely make a living.

· · ·

"Can you fly out tomorrow?" I asked Sam over the phone.

"I don't know, man. Maybe. I'll have to see."

"See?"

"Dude, I'm gonna go, okay. Chill out. I just don't know when yet. I've gotta to talk to my boss. He's a pain in my ass, and work's been nuts."

I always challenged Sam, which he of course hated. But I couldn't lose him at this juncture, so I backed off.

After college, Sam had interviewed for a marketing and sales position in Minnesota. He got the job and fled Texas just as soon. Three years and a promotion later, he was clearing a decent salary. He'd bought a new Corvette and lived in a spiffy little condo suited for his bachelor lifestyle.

The problem was his boss. Sam said his boss only cared about accounts and the bottom line. If Sam were to ask to take a sudden leave of absence, his future with the company would likely be compromised.

In the wake of Mom's death, Sam's situation was complete bullshit, but I tried to understand. I always tried. The Dude needed someone to give him breaks.

"All right, well, fly out this weekend then," I snapped. "We'll figure it out when you get here. Mom ain't going anywhere."

"Dude, don't say it like that."

"Sorry."

"I'll let you know when I get the tickets."

"Okay. Hey, one more thing."

"What?"

"Quit that fucking job already," I said. "I think Santa has enough helpers."

"Kiss my ass."

• • •

Our last conversation had been on the phone, maybe a week ago.

"How's work?" Mom had asked me.

"Good," I'd replied.

Good was my answer for most of Mom's questions when we chatted on the phone. I cultivated that response to keep our conversations short and sweet. Everything was always *good* even if it wasn't.

We'd do our real catching up in person.

Our final conversation ended with, "I love you." On the phone or face-to-face, that's always how we left off.

Even though we lived in the same city, we went weeks without seeing each other. When too much time had passed, Catholic guilt would get the best of me and I'd call her for dinner.

I sat in the waiting room and tried to hear her voice in my head, the only place it would exist now. There was maybe a home movie from when Dad was still around, but it was probably somewhere collecting dust in a cardboard box.

. . .

Dad was great until he walked out on us when I was seven years old. He worked nights as a grocery warehouse supervisor at H-E-B and on his days off, he took Sam and me to the movies where he'd fall asleep.

Dad wrestled with us, took us fishing and talked Mom into letting us stay up late on weekends, if we behaved. He handed us stacks of quarters at the mall arcade and taught us how to shoot baskets.

I remember his red work polos and his Tom Selleck mustache prickling my head when he kissed the top of it. Dad was strong, quiet.

I remember wanting to be just like him.

. . .

When Dad was stressed out, which was every day after he got off work, he'd come home and drink. When they were still together, Mom sipped, but Dad drank.

For some people, alcohol brings out aggression and hostility; others, silliness and stupor. With Dad, a crapshoot. Every so often, his drunkenness plunged him into a dark world where no one could be trusted. One wrong word and you were in his sights.

With somebody like that, here's what eventually happens.

One night, when Mom and Dad had decided to stay in, there wasn't enough countertop space in the kitchen for him to place his empty Budweiser cans. They spilled onto the floor.

Dad was in that dark world. Mom was his only target.

A shouting match ensued.

"You're so fucking sloppy!" Mom yelled.

Dad must've heard something worse.

"What did you say to me, you whiny bitch?"

Things got physical. Mom pushed him; he pushed her back.

She slapped his face; he punched hers. She fell onto the kitchen floor.

I was kneeling behind the sofa near the kitchen to eavesdrop and watch. I had crawled out of bed after they'd woken me up. I heard the hollow thud of Mom's body hit the kitchen linoleum. I felt the impact on my knees.

Dad stumbled out of the kitchen to the front door. I was in the fetal position, terrified he'd find me. He opened the door and slammed it so hard the whole house shook. I heard his truck speed off and that was that. We never saw him again, at least I didn't. I crawled over to Mom, who was sprawled on the floor, bleeding from her head.

. . .

I talked with doctors and told them I'd decide what to do with her later. I just needed out for a little while. They said okay, do what I needed to do.

On my drive back to my apartment, I thought about nothing.

When I got to my place, a smelly dump with cracked and yellowed drywalls and grimy carpet pockmarked with irremovable stains, my mind caved in. I suddenly felt terribly lonely.

I grabbed my cell to call Marcela. I wanted to tell her everything. Wanted to hear her voice. But my fingers wouldn't dial her number.

After five years of what I'd thought was a great ride, I caught her in our bed with some beefcake she'd met while working at the hospital. Marcela was a nurse and made twice as much as me, so she kept the quaint place we shared on the north central side of town—the nice side.

"Have fun fucking John Cena," were the last words I said to her.

She said nothing back, only wept into her hands.

I lived in a shithole I called my own. I lived on Maruchan Ramen and Chef Boyardee. I lived like a champ.

. . .

I stood with Sam on the driveway of the small, one-story home on Lucky Drive. The house we grew up in looked so old to me, as it always had. As a kid, I remember being embarrassed by the bright blue wooden panels—a light Mexican blue Mom had picked out that faded into a lighter, uglier shade each passing year.

The house would be left to me, but in that moment, I hadn't yet thought about the finer points of Texas intestate succession laws or even what to do with Mom's body. Later, I'd decide to have it cremated.

Sam scanned the pavement. I was certain he was recalling all the one-on-one we'd played and how I whooped his ass every game.

"Has it really been three years?" he asked.

We stood in silence for a minute.

"So your boss was cool with you getting away?" I asked.

"Hell naw. He gave me shit like I told you."

"And what'd you say back? Please tell me you pushed back."

"I told him, 'Kiss my ass, Kris Kringle.'"

We cracked smiles. It was the best thing I'd heard in a while.

Then Sam reached into the front pocket of his blue jeans and pulled out a joint and a Bic lighter.

"How the hell did you sneak that onto the plane?" I asked.

"I didn't, dummy," he answered.

Sam held the roach between his lips, cupped his left hand over it while he lit it with his right, then took a long, deep hit, eyes closed, exhaled a cloud of white smoke into the warm summer air.

Even-Steven

∞

Will Valdez parked his car far enough from the cliff's edge. His brother waited there, leaning against his pickup truck, hands in his jean pockets, gazing at the small patch of city in the blue South Texas horizon.

Will got out of his car and shuffled slowly toward his brother. He felt nothing the closer he got. He hesitated before raising his hand to shake his brother's. It was quick.

"Good to see you, Willie."

"You too, Steve."

They looked at each other for a while before Steve pointed to the cliff's edge and said, "Let's go sit over there."

Will peered down and noticed the trees and boulders and rocks far below.

Helluva place to meet, he thought.

The brothers sat down and let their legs dangle.

"Remember when Pops used to take us to the valley and we'd run around Tía Nora's yard?" Steve asked softly.

"Yeah."

"The way the sky's all blue and shit, kinda reminds me of that."

Steve smiled. Will didn't.

"So, how's business? Still making the big bucks, Mr. Insurance Man?" Steve patted Will's back, a peace offering.

"Not yet," Will answered.

"You'll get there someday."

"Hopefully."

Awkward silence.

"Well, yer prolly wondering why I asked you to meet me out here in the middle of fuckin' nowhere." Steve sounded amused.

Will wanted to say, "No shit, Sherlock." When he'd Googled Sombra Cliff and saw how far he'd have to drive, his first thought was, Fucking seriously?

"They taught me lots of stuff while I was in rehab, bro. Stuff I wish I woulda known a long time ago. They said having conversations outdoors, places like here, helps the natural energy flow of the body, or some shit. Basically all yer stimulis get activated so it's easier to talk. Sounds gay, I know, but I thought it seemed cool."

"Good view," Will said blandly. He noticed Steve's stupid smile fade a bit.

"Yessir," Steve agreed.

If you looked into the blue South Texas horizon, you'd see a watery wave. The July air hot and still. The water in the ravine below Sombra Cliff had dried up months before, when warm air currents from the Mexican deserts blew north. For the latter half of the year, the land surrounding Sombra Cliff hardly saw a drop of rain.

Will didn't want to be there. That much was obvious. The back of his T-shirt was already damp. Having a wet back, literally, made him think of childhood, and he wasn't in any mood to think about that.

"Look man, first I wanna say thanks for coming out here. I know the drive probably took you a while, so I appreciate that. But I don't wanna waste yer time, so I'll stop bullshitting."

Will saw Steve shift his body some. He'd already anticipated what his brother was about to say. He'd rehearsed this act in his head.

"I've been thinking a lot about the accident, bro, about being in rehab and—look, I fucked up, man. I fucked up real bad."

Steve cleared his throat. The word "accident" hit Will's ears like a hammer. It wasn't an accident.

"Sorry, bro. This is hard for me."

"Keep going," Will said sharply.

Steve registered the coldness in his brother's voice. For a second, he didn't think he'd be able to continue. Maybe this was a bad idea after all. He looked up at the sky, closed his eyes and drew a deep breath. He'd get through this. He needed to. He owed his big brother that much.

"I know yer fuckin' pissed. I get that. But I've done a lot of what they call self-reflection. I've thought a lot about things lately. I wanna talk to you cuz yer my blood, and they told me the more I talk to people I'm close with the more vulnerable I become. And being vulnerable is good, I guess. For healing and shit. Maybe it'll help you heal, too."

Will's raw anger stage had long since passed. Inside, he felt he'd already been reduced to a black hole, though on the outside he was twenty pounds fatter in fast food weight. He couldn't remember the last home-cooked meal he'd enjoyed, but he remembered the last meal she'd cooked. Chicken parmesan with green beans and mashed potatoes. She hated mashed potatoes, but he'd insisted. Will also remembered—he couldn't forget—how in the mornings, before he left to work, she'd always leave him two pieces of toast. The idea of having toast now was unfathomable. He remembered how on Sunday mornings, before church, Julie would sometimes whip him up scrambled eggs and bacon. They hardly missed Sunday mass, but after she died, Will stopped going. He couldn't manage seeing other people live their happy little lives, and he definitely couldn't be around babies. The idea of starting his own family was like a fairy tale now. He could no longer listen to Father O'Reilly, with his salt-and-pepper hair and thick-framed Ray-Ban glasses. He couldn't stand to listen to another word about Jesus' love for humanity, about anything unless he goddamn felt like it.

At the office, Will became a bigger workhorse. He'd used his risk management degree to work his way up in auto insurance, save good money and start his own business, WillCo. He managed a small team. He intended to keep the business growing, even with Julie gone—especially with her gone.

Once the life of the party at work, Will was now cold. Removed. After Julie died, his team had bought him a bouquet of flowers and signed a card for him. Even JoAnna Vernon, the tall, slender brunette, had offered to stay with Will at his home, but he said no. He shut everyone down. He locked himself in his office, and at home. Now that Will no longer had a fiancé to go home to and to love and to make love to, it was just him. He'd fully grasped what that meant until he was numb, reduced to a stub, a black hole. Everything in, nothing out.

Will was not, however, above getting irritated. His mother called him frequently. He answered sparingly, worrying her. She'd already had enough to worry about with Steve.

"Just get it off your chest, Steve," Will snapped.

Steve's lips started to move, and that's when Will noticed a long hair sticking out on Steve's otherwise freshly shaven upper lip—a hair that curled into his mouth.

Steve talked about the night of the accident, how nothing like that had ever happened before, how Julie—who'd been studying for the bar exam—told him to stay in after he finished his last beer. Steve acknowledged how goddamn stubborn he was, how motherfucking selfless she was to not let her own brother-in-law go out drunk.

What Steve really wanted to get off his chest, though, was how he wished it had been him—not her—who had flown into the lamppost.

Julie didn't have her seatbelt on. She was ejected through the windshield. Will would never know how she'd actually tried to put on her seatbelt but couldn't since the buckle was jammed. He'd never gotten around to fixing it.

Julie's skull caved in. Steve came away with only a mild concussion. Somehow, come to find out, he was buckled in.

That night, Will stayed late at the office and went out for drinks afterwards. He'd planned on going home, but JoAnna Vernon convinced him otherwise.

Steve's apology-laced retelling was something Will had already heard before, in his head. So all he actually heard coming out of his brother's mouth now was *yadda yadda yadda*.

There were a few details Steve left out.

From the time Steve first met Julie at a Valdez family barbecue, back when he was still in high school, he'd enjoyed the eyes he thought she'd given him. Steve was happy-go-lucky, more so than Will. When he'd crack a good joke in front of Julie, she'd touch the sides of his arms gently, and he'd tap her waist, strum her as if she was his guitar.

Will had picked up on this one time. When he brought it up to Julie, she told him to knock it off, that obviously, she was not that kind of girl.

• • •

Steve enjoyed attention from women the same way he enjoyed beer—one sip and he wanted the whole thing.

He first tasted beer when he was six years old. His father, after getting home from work late one night, called him and Will to join him on the sofa. He showed the boys his twenty-four ounce can of Schlitz.

"A little sip won't hurt nobody," their father had said.

Will sipped, made a sour face. Steve sipped, licked his lips.

The night of Steve's twenty-first birthday, he was charged for public intoxication. He spent the night in jail, and the next day, Will picked him up.

"What the hell's the matter with you?" Will said.

Steve didn't acknowledge the question. He kept his eyes on the road.

"Hello?"

"What?"

Will drove for another minute before reengaging.

"Mom's worried about you, dude. You know what she said?"

"Naw."

"Well, I'm going to tell you. She said maybe we're still cursed. She said she thought it was over after Dad left, but now she's not so sure anymore. She's scared for you, dude. She's really scared."

Steve stayed quiet, clenched his fists.

"You going to keep this shit up?" Will said.

"Don't you ever just shut the fuck up?"

"What'd you say me to me?"

Steve yawned. Will couldn't believe the diss.

"All right, Steve," he said. "See if I bail your ass out next time."

"Don't worry, bro. Ma will," Steve said. He regretted his cruelty the rest of the ride.

A year later, Steve was hired at the post office. He wasn't sure how, but to have an honest government job at age twenty-two was pretty damn cool, he thought. An accomplishment.

He delivered mail for six years. Then, after a week of showing up late, he was fired. It was the hangovers after the breakup with Beckah. Steve had dated Beckah for a year and a half, his first real girlfriend. She wore black fishnet stockings, had a tattoo sleeve of a green and red dragon and proudly smacked her Juicy Fruit gum. What Steve enjoyed best about Beckah was the sex; what Beckah enjoyed best about Steve was hard to say. One day, without explaining herself, Beckah left Steve. Moved in with another guy. At first Steve acted like he didn't give a shit, but when he realized he actually did, thinking about the night they stared into each other's eyes a whole five minutes without a word, then her whispering she could imagine being with him the rest of her life because he wasn't anything like her father, and that they should start reading Jane Austen and Sartre together, he turned to old faithful. After five days of showing up late for work, it didn't help Steve's case that his supervisor, Maureen, a middle-aged woman whose heart had been stomped on by drug addicts most of her life, never bothered to ask him if something was wrong. She needed a reason to fire Steve, and she got one. Case closed.

No job, no girlfriend, and with rent due that'd gobble up his last paycheck, Steve was forced to text Will. Julie responded to him, assuring him that they'd help him land back on his feet, no problem.

When Will told Steve over the phone that the condition through which he could stay with them was that he quit drinking until he found a job, Steve accepted begrudgingly. Getting a job wouldn't be a problem, he thought; going cold turkey would. Steve really didn't want to live with his brother, follow his rules, but at this juncture in his life, he didn't have much choice.

But there was Julie.

Bumming around his brother's house while he was away at work, Steve couldn't help but keep track of Julie's where-abouts, her movements—watching her strut around in her yoga pants. He had to look.

One day, while Julie was in the kitchen making a pot of coffee for a long study session, Steve went to grab a glass of water. When his hand brushed her butt, he didn't say a word, just waited. To his relief, she said nothing as well. Gave him eyes.

Some seeds need just a little bit of watering, Steve thought. Even though I know I'll chainsaw the tree down.

A week later, on an evening when Will was working late, Steve and Julie made out on the sofa. She grabbed him there. Or rather he positioned her hand there. He lifted her and carried her to the bathroom and propped her on the coun-tertop. He stripped off her shirt, then her pants. She stopped him and said she was so sorry and then ran off to her bed-room and slammed the door.

Steve stood there, recalling his philosophy about the seeds. How some needed just a little more watering than others. And how someday the tree would fall.

• • •

As the brothers sat on the cliff's edge, their shirts drenched in sweat, Steve's heart pounded. He felt it in his Adam's apple.

"Look, bro," he said, "what I'm trying to say is—I'm sorry about Julie. I'm sorry about everything."

There it was. Hearing her name out of his mouth jolted Will more than expected.

Steve felt outside his body.

Will heard a flock of birds screaming in the distance.

"Don't apologize," Will said.

"I have to."

Seeing the entire city from a distance gyrate like a watery worm was a peculiar experience for Will. The blistering heat overstimulating.

He looked below the cliff's edge, then back up at his brother. He felt almost sorry for him.

"Remember the time in Corpus when Dad took us to Tío David's and Tío David gave us the Mexican Cokes? The ones in the bottle?" Steve asked.

"Yeah."

"I picked some up on the way over here. Want one?"

"You know, that sounds like a great idea," Will answered.

"Okay, lemme grab 'em."

Will needed a quick break from all this, even if just for a minute.

"No, I'll go get them," he said.

"I got it, bro."

"No."

Steve tried reading his big brother's face but couldn't. He said, "All right," then handed Will his keys.

"They're in the back of the truck, in the cooler," Steve said.

"Cool."

Will walked slowly to Steve's truck. He counted his steps—twenty-three.

He hopped in the bed and admired the aluminum cooler shining in the sunlight. He opened it and plunged his hand into the ice.

"Goddamn," he muttered.

He turned toward his brother, who seemed to be sitting on the cliff's edge serenely, motionless, a Buddha.

Will bent down to close the cooler and glanced inside the back window of the truck.

The knot in his stomach grew as big as a basketball. It wasn't a knot so much as a churning of guts.

Will couldn't take his eyes off the three silver beer cans by the gas pedal, crushed from the middle. Empty Schlitz cans from the look of it, the same kind he used to find on his kitchen table in the morning when Steve still lived with them.

"Here you go," Will said, handing an opened glass bottle of Coke to his little brother.

Still seated, Steve grabbed the Coke and smiled.

"Thanks," he said.

Will, standing behind Steve, took a hearty swig of Coke and thought about the polar bears in the commercials, about how happy and stupid they looked.

"You gonna sit?" Steve asked.

The gyrating worm of the blue horizon. Will considered how even the biggest things appear as Lego blocks if you stood far enough away.

For a second, he saw a beautiful woman in the trees. She waved at him, as if to say, "Come on down here."

"Hello?"

To Steve, Will seemed as though he were deep in prayer, but he knew he wasn't.

Steve could no longer talk. Couldn't move. For the first time since they'd sat down, he realized how close to down there he was. The trees and boulders and rocks far below.

He'd never believed in curses or in any of that Mexican crap grandmothers spewed. But now—all of it. Every last story.

Will placed both his hands on Steve's shoulders. Steve felt the rage in his brother's fingers as they dug into his clavicles. His legs shook uncontrollably. The rest of his body, too.

Then, Will was beside him, seated.

Breathless—indebted—Steve hugged his brother, hugged him hard. Cried.

"What's wrong with you?" Will asked.

Steve was unable to respond. Will's sudden back-slap had startled him, inched him forward. Will kept his hand smack dab in the middle of his wet back.

Peering into Steve's wide wet eyes, the almost-gone look behind his pupils, Will felt for the first time in weeks, months, that he was in control. This is how it's going to be, he thought. Only the beginning.

He lowered his hand from his little brother's back and grabbed his Coke, took another big swig, let out a sigh. The burn in his throat felt good.

Pancakes and Waffles

∞

I sat across from Columbia at IHOP and gazed into her cocoa eyes. They were like two shiny, brown M&Ms. I could've stared at them all night. Sorceress of a blonde, I thought. My stomach tingled.

I've got nothing against blonde-haired, blue-eyed girls, but they're to be expected. Run of the mill, as my mother would say. But blonde-haired, brown-eyed girls? They're a different breed of beast, as my father would say. Life for them, I imagined, was an uphill battle. Victims of fate, the lot of them—prisoners of predetermination. I'm inclined to call them underdogs. But let's get one thing straight about Columbia: she was no underdog.

"What're you looking at?" she asked.

"Nothing," I lied.

"You were looking at me really weird."

"I'm sorry. Your eyes, they're pretty."

She smiled and said, "I know, right?"

Her teeth were perfect: pure white, immaculate. I could tell she never skipped a day brushing them.

She scooted her body further inside the booth, her collar-bones showing through her V-neck.

I thought, What I really want to do is reach across and ...

"Why're you still staring at me?"

"I'm not," I lied.

* * *

I was a sophomore in college when I ran into Columbia pretty much by pure chance. After graduating from high school, two years chugged along, then one day while I was on my lunch break at the mall—I worked at Dillard's—there she was in the food court. I didn't realize I'd cut three people in line at Subway to say hi to her. Actually, I'm lying.

"Jerk," I heard a woman mutter. I waved at her friendly.

Then Columbia turned around and squealed. "Oh my God!"

"Yes, it is I," I said, and we bear-hugged.

After she paid for her sandwich, we sat down at a table and small-talked a bit, both of us all smiles. The whole time I kept wondering, Why isn't your number in my phone? When we hit a stopping point, I asked for it casually.

Then I said, "Would you like to go to dinner sometime?" Because why not. Because pure chance.

"Dinner?" she repeated.

"Yeah, like, can I take you to dinner? Unless you're busy or something."

"Whoa. Take me to dinner. That sounds like a serious proposal, good sir."

I stayed quiet, unsure how to respond.

Finally, she said, "I'm messing with you, dork. Of course we can 'go to dinner.'" The last part in a deeper voice as if to mimic mine.

"Great! Well, now that I have your number, I can call you soon?"

"Sounds bueno, señor!"

I waited two days—carefully planned.

"Hey," I said over the phone, "how does IHOP sound, Friday night?"

"Um, yeah, sure, IHOP sounds ... cool," Columbia answered.

To me, IHOP was a more respectable option than McDonald's, and much more affordable than somewhere overrated like Outback Steakhouse, which, on my budget, was totally out of the question.

"I can pick you up, if you'd like?"

There was a little bit of static, then she said, "Yeah, sounds good."

"I mean, if it's okay with y—"

"I said yes, silly. Come grab me at six."

After we hung up, I got on MapQuest and mapped her address. It was a forty-five-minute drive from my dorm to her place. The damn girl lives in Djibouti, I thought.

When I arrived at her neighborhood, I was surprised to find myself in a trailer park in Devine, thirty miles outside the city. I had no clue she lived in a trailer park.

She was standing outside her home, looking criminally fine in dark blue jeans and a low-cut T-shirt imprinted with a faded American flag.

Suddenly, an image of her—draped in an American flag, Old Glory, nothing else on underneath—popped in my head, and I quickly brushed away the wicked fantasy, if such a thing were possible.

"I had no idea you lived in a trailer park," I said. I had no idea how horrendous those words sounded until they escaped my trap.

"I mean, I wasn't trying to say—"

"It's all good," Columbia said curtly. "This is where I dwell. Surprise!"

"Hey, you look great," I said, changing the subject.

"Not bad for a trailer-park girl, huh?" she said, grinning like Satan himself and my face heating up.

"I'm messing with you. Why so serious?"

"I'm not," I said defensively, childishly. Then I high-fived her to play it off. Amateur move.

On the drive to IHOP, we small-talked, and at some point I played music from my iPod. I'd created a playlist for our date. Columbia and I had both loved the same bands in high school. Green Day, Death Cab for Cutie, Dashboard Confessional, Panic! At The Disco, all of them. Thus, I'd titled my playlist, "Columbia Records." When I showed her, she looked at me with her melted M&M glowing eyes.

We walked inside IHOP and an ancient waitress named Doris greeted us at the counter. I counted legit ten thousand wrinkles on her face. She asked us if we wanted a table or a booth, and I said booth, so Doris shepherded us to one slowly—oh so slowly. She called the both of us "honey" in a refined smoker's voice. From the look on her face, Columbia was as amused as I was.

After Doris shuffled off to give us some time, Columbia said, breaking a smile, "Stop being mean."

"I'm not being mean at all ... *honey*!"

"God, don't start!"

"Seriously, how many packs of Camel do you think that woman's put away in her lifetime?"

"You're evil," Columbia said, grinning like Lucifer.

When Doris came back, Columbia's stern gaze seemed to order me, *Don't you dare do it.*

She ordered chocolate-chip pancakes.

"And I'll have the Belgian waffle with scrambled eggs," I said to Doris in a heavy smoker's voice. I couldn't believe I'd just imitated her right to her wrinkled face. With Columbia around, the court jester in me seemed to bumble out.

By a miracle of God, Doris seemed bothered not one iota by my sophomoric stunt. I was a sophomore, after all. And, after all, she had lived through several world-shaping wars, Eisenhower and Tricky Dick. She'd probably had a litter of children, all grown now. And lots of grandchildren. Me? I was just another punk-ass kid she had to serve on a Friday night in hopes of earning a halfway-decent tip. Back then, I lacked the decency to tip decently.

Columbia, she kicked me good in the shin.

The food arrived in a blink. My eggs were warm and fluffy. The waffle practically melted in my mouth, as if, texturally speaking, it was one and the same as the butter I'd spread across it affectionately like a Bob Ross brushstroke. *Oh look, a happy little butter cloud.*

I scarfed down everything fast like a wolf. Columbia had only taken a few bites of her pancakes by the time I finished.

"Cowabunga," she said. "You weren't that hungry, huh?"

"Nah," I replied. "I hated every bite."

I could only watch as Columbia ate and, surprisingly, she didn't make a stink about my food voyeurism. She chewed each bite like twenty times, real methodical. Her lips stayed closed shut, all mannered. I imagined her looking up at me and saying, Not too bad for a trailer-park girl, huh?

In between chews, Columbia said she'd been attending community college, which, in this town, translated to a Venus fly-trap for high school slackers. Columbia said she'd also been working part-time at a children's daycare. She loved the job but hated going to school at the same time and was considering taking a year off. College was too much like high school, she said. I wanted to tell her right then and there to not unenroll, to just stick with it. Otherwise, she'd never go back. But I didn't say anything. I just nodded my head and listened.

"And you?" she asked. "You planning to graduate on time?"

"That's the plan," I answered. "Two more years and I should have that degree in my greedy little hands."

"Right on! You've always been smart like that."

Her comment rubbed me the wrong way. I'd always felt I did exactly what I was supposed to do. Really, I felt, I was no smarter than her.

I broke up our serious talk by doing an impression of Michael Scott from *The Office*. Why? Because Columbia and I had both talked about loving *The Office* in high school. Because we were the coolest nerds and had immaculate taste. And because I was highly skilled at impressions. No one greater.

"Would I rather be feared or loved? Easy. Both. I want people to be afraid of how much they love me," I intoned as Steve Carrell.

Columbia almost spat the last of her pancakes in my face.

"Oh my God, yes!" she said, pointing at my mouth. "That's amazing! And that episode was the fucking shiz!"

Doris returned to pick up our plates and I noticed she had the sourest expression I'd ever witnessed on a human face. At least, one as copiously wrinkled as hers.

"You're a doll," I said to Doris in Doris-voice. Oops! I did it again, I thought in Britney Spears' voice.

"Aren't you the sweetest lil' honey," Doris replied, unleashing a frightening smile revealing missing teeth—holes that'd snugly fit multiple cigarettes.

Before I could clown again, Columbia kicked both my shins. Pop-pop! She clearly had a soft spot for old geezers.

As we waited for our check—though we'd soon figure out that we were to pay at the register near the entrance—I glanced around the restaurant. Except for an elderly couple sitting behind us, there was nobody else in the house. The graveyard shift had begun. People, it seemed, had better things to do on a Friday night.

I turned back toward Columbia and caught her picking her teeth with her pointer finger.

"Oh my God, don't judge me," she said. "I get food stuck all the time."

"I'm not judging," I lied.

"This is like, totally inappropriate of me to ask, but, can you check to see if there's anything else in there?"

"Gladly," I replied.

She flashed her perfectly straight, immaculately white chompers at me. The girl oughta be in damn toothpaste commercials, I thought.

"Let's see what we've got," I said officiously.

I focused in on one of her Chiclets. "Houston, we've got a problem."

Columbia's hand shot to her mouth.

"Shut up! For real?"

"You'd better go take a gander. Something big's wedged in there."

"Oh my God!"

She quickly slid out of the booth and, as she got up and zipped off to the restroom, I thought, What an ass—myself. I'd never felt this way toward her back in high school. At least, I didn't think so. My stomach tingled.

When she returned, she playfully punched my arm.

"You freakin' jerk," she said.

"I'm gonna press assault charges on you."

"You deserve a good kick in the gonads, too."

"Usually, always."

The elderly couple behind us—I glanced back at them again—collectively glared at me. They found nothing about me or our company charming. Perhaps we'd disturbed the final moments of their peace on Earth. For a quick second, I pictured Columbia and me as them, past our primes, past our expiration dates. Cottage cheese that used to be milk.

I nodded at them and they snapped their heads away in the same direction, kind of like angry turtles.

"What the heck are you doing now?"

"Twelve o'clock, right behind me," I whispered. "Don't make it obvious."

Columbia snuck a peek at the couple, then said to me, discreetly, "Evil, evil man."

Suddenly, her expression changed. It was as though she contemplated something heavy, wretched. A black cloud had dulled the shine of her M&Ms.

"You know," she said, "I love old people. I really do. But they make me sad for whatever reason."

"What'd you mean?" I said, legit confused.

"Like, doesn't it suck to know that's it's all gonna end sooner than we think?"

She snapped her fingers.

"What'd you mean?" I pressed.

"Okay, like, here's life," she said, holding out her hands about a foot apart from each other, palms facing inward. "You live for all this stuff in between, then before you know it, we're here," she said, shaking her right hand.

I was taken aback.

"What the hell did they put in your pancakes?" I said. "Did you go and snort something in the bathroom? A little coke, you diabolical wench?"

Columbia didn't smile.

"I'm kidding, I'm kidding," I said, straightening my back. "Look, I think the point of life is to enjoy all the in-between stuff—really enjoy it—so that when this comes," I said, shaking my right hand, "you're good with it. You're cool with it. At peace. Capisce?"

Columbia looked out the window, to a mostly dead parking lot.

"Yeah," she answered softly. "I guess it's just ... I don't know, I just see things differently. It's hard to explain. I don't really enjoy all the in-between stuff knowing the end's coming. I've always thought this way. I enjoy things to a certain point, and then I don't. I love going to the movies. I love watching people do weird shit in the snack line. I love the smell of movie popcorn. I love picking out the perfect seats in the dark. But at the end of the day, all the lights come on and I have to go back home. Then before we know it all the lights shut off for good. Do you see what I'm saying? I don't know ... I should just stop talking now."

I wanted to bust out another Michael Scott impression, but it was like the water in my funny well had dried up. I had to dig us out of there, and pronto.

"Listen," I said. "I get what you mean. I totally do. But I think when things're going well, when you're having a good time, just stop and enjoy the moment. Like right now, for instance. Let's both take a second to enjoy how dumb you looked with all that pancake in your mouth."

The edges of her lips curled up.

"You know what else there, lil' lady?" I added. "Sometimes you make my noodle spin like a lasso at the rodeo, so I'sa reckon you knock it off and we hit that ol' dusty trail." My Hollywood Cowboy accent was always a hoot at parties.

"In case you've never been mandated," Columbia said, smiling, "you need to have your head examined. As of yesterday."

If I'd had the ability to freeze time, the minute that followed is the moment I'd've frozen. Comfortable silence, satisfied stomachs, infinite possibilities everywhere.

"Just so you know, I baffle everyone," Columbia said, breaking our mutual quiet. "That's probably why I don't have lots of friends. People think they know me, but they really don't. I guess that's my schtick."

"Your schtick?" I said.

"Yep. My schtick. Funny word, ain't it? Schtick."

"Schtick is a goofy word," I agreed.

• • • •

At the cash register, I told Doris to put it on one check.

"It's okay, I'll pay my half," Columbia said, reaching inside her purse. I gently grabbed her wrist.

"I got it," I said.

"No, it's okay, but thank you."

"No, it's not okay. I got it."

"One check or two?" Doris said impatiently. My earlier charisma counted for squat.

"One check," I answered definitively.

Columbia squeezed me hard in the area where a love handle hadn't yet grown.

In my ear, she whispered, "Jerk."

My stomach tingled.

. . .

There wasn't much small talk on the drive back, so I put on the same playlist we'd heard earlier. The Ramones. The Sex Pistols. Rancid. Black Flag. The Clash. blink-182.

"What a Wonderful World" by Louis Armstrong weirdly slipped into the mix, and Columbia sucked in a deep breath and remarked, rather remarkably: "Who stops to listen to music anymore? Like, who lets it call to them?" Then another genre outlier infiltrated the party, Amy Winehouse's "You Know I'm No Good," to which we sang together loudly the part where Amy says *And sniffed me out like I was Tanqueray.*

When we got back to her place, it was pitch dark outside. All the lights were off everywhere. For all I knew, I was in another country. I practically was: in Devine, the hill country. Country living. A different breed of beast, I heard in my father's voice.

Then I remembered in high school when, during a lunch, Columbia confessed that her mom had grounded her once for two months because she forgot to bathe her baby sister. I did the math quickfire: two months was one-sixth of a year. I realized how Columbia had only mentioned bad things about her family. It didn't seem to me, then, that a girl like her could come from a family like hers.

"Thanks for tonight," she said. "And for paying for me. That was really sweet."

"No problem," I said. "I had lots of fun."

Though I could barely make out her face—I'd killed the headlights when I got to her trailer—the moonlight painted a shape I knew belonged only to her.

I put my hand to my chest, felt my heart pound. Then she spoke again.

"Y'know," she said, "I never did thank you that time you lent me your shirt junior year."

"What?" I blurted.

"Your shirt, junior year, remember? So I wouldn't get expelled?"

"I mean, yes, I remember that. I'm just wondering what made you think of that right now?"

"Well, because I hadn't thanked you before, and now, I'm

taking the opportunity to do so. See how this works, good sir?"

"No, it's just ... you baffle me. You do baffle me. I suppose this proves I'm exactly like everyone else."

Her moonlit mouth formed a smile.

"Don't you remember you kissed me on the cheek outside the computer lab? How could you forget that?" I said.

"I kissed you?"

"Yeah. On the cheek."

"Dang. You're right. How could I forget that?"

"Harsh. You'll make a great public defender someday."

"Wiseass," she said.

"Show you a wiseass," I said. A dare, sort of.

There was silence—less comfortable this time.

After a while—I don't know how long—Columbia said, "Mr. Jenkins would've kicked me out of school. Mom would've murdered me. All for a lousy blouse. I didn't even have boobs. I still don't."

"We all knew Mr. Jenkins had a hard-on for you," I said, try-ing—failing—not to think about her chest. "He just wanted you to gush on his porn 'stache."

"Barf, that's gross even to joke about. I'd rather die."

"Hey, everything turned out all right, didn't it?"

Outside my window, I saw the dark mass that was Columbia's home. Inside was her mother—her mother, in bed fast asleep, or perhaps waiting for her rebellious daughter to step inside so she could lock her up in her room. One-sixth of a year.

"Well," Columbia said, breaking my impure imaginings, "I'd better get going."

"Alrighty."

"Call me again sometime?"

"For sure," I said. "I've got your digits now."

When our eyes met, different information was passed along. Damaging, is how I came to later think about it. My heart pounded through my throat. I felt all of its vitality. My brain drilled a single command into me, repeated it over and over.

Do it. Do it. Do it now.

I put my hand on her lap—she didn't remove it. My other hand went to her chin and raised it. Her breathing heavy, labored.

Then she pushed my seat back, climbed on top of me.

She clasped my face, bit my bottom lip soft, then hard. My hands slid up her shirt, then down.

She seized my hands and said, "Nah ah."

Gripping both my hands, she forced them south, slowly, her control, her pace. She leaned into my ear and it was all hot breath.

"Good boy," she whispered.

Some things you promise to keep to yourself your whole life. What happened then is one of them.

. . .

Back in my car, windows fogged up, Columbia smoothed her hair looking into the passenger mirror, our vision having adjusted to the dark.

Silent, I studied her slender fingers slide across her curls as if she was playing the harp.

When she flipped the mirror up, she said, "See ya later, alligator."

"In a while, crocodile," I said back.

She stepped out of my car and walked toward her front door, never turning around to wave goodbye. I couldn't know what this would mean to me in the years to come.

I waited a few seconds, hoping she'd come back to send me off with a kiss. But no. There was nothing left for me to do. So I left.

Not once on the drive back did I peer at my rearview mirror.
Not once did I play any music.

I drove.

. . .

I waited for a call, a text. None arrived. Three days in a row I
texted a single question mark. Three question marks stacked
one on top of the other. All unanswered. Soon, her voicemail message disappeared, replaced by a repulsive robotic
voice informing me that the person's voicemail inbox was
full. Sorry, goodbye. Basically, I never heard from her again.
Not really.

. . .

Quick sidenote: These days, whenever a song comes on from
say, blink-182, Green Day, Panic! At The Disco—bands of my
adolescence, basically, of the pop-punk variety—I listen to it
with an initial pleasure that rapidly fades, as though seeing
an old friend whose irritating habits the passage of time
made me forget.

For the record, I never finished watching *The Office* in its
entirety. I saw maybe the first three seasons and then in
college got hooked on these new-at-the-time shows called
Breaking Bad and *Mad Men.* Maybe you've heard of them?
Good stuff.

Also—and sorry to leave this on a downer—one day during
my last year of college, I was scrolling through local news
articles when I read, to my complete shock, that Mr. Jenkins,

my principal in high school, was caught having an inappropriate relationship with a seventeen-year-old girl. He shot himself in the head, having felt, I assumed, he'd flushed his life down the toilet. My first thought, though I'm ashamed to admit it, was this: I bid thee adieu, Mr. Porn 'Stache. What my former principal did with—to—that girl is absolutely disgusting. Unquestionably immoral. But knowing how his story ended makes me sick to my stomach. Just plain sad. I occasionally think about the wife and son he left behind. If they're okay. If like the rest of us they manage to, on occasion, enjoy good meals and lively music, despite all the terrors.

. . .

After graduating from college, I saw this girl named Priscilla. She was short, dark, round-faced, opinionated—a braggadocious Catholic, basically. We'd met in undergrad but didn't know each other well.

A superficial game of twenty-one questions on Facebook led to me asking her out to dinner. Easy-peasy.

On our first date, I remember her saying, "If I ever caught my husband watching porn, I'd throw that pig out of my life so hard his balls would spin."

When you're younger, red flags don't mean as much.

We lasted a few months, Priscilla and I. Did all the things young people do fresh out of college. One night, I'd planned to pick her up at her apartment so we could go out for a steak dinner. I'd earned a small bonus at work. I'd made reservations two weeks in advance. When I got to her place, I called but she didn't answer. I called twice more and still no answer. I waited a few minutes before trying again. Straight to voice-mail. I don't know how long I was out there stalling, my cologne seeping into my nostrils. Fed up, I sped off.

Halfway home, she called me back.

"I'm sooo sorry!" she said in a panic. "I totally crashed after I got home from work. I'm sorry!"

"Alrighty," I said.

"You're not mad, are you?"

"Why would I be mad, Priscilla?"

"Hey, like, I'm really sorry, okay."

"Don't be. You're tired, right? So rest up. Have a good night."

She immediately called back.

"You hung up on me? Like, seriously?"

"What'd you want me to say?" I said.

"You know what? All right then." Click.

I called back and it was straight to voicemail.

That night, I had a wild dream. I don't remember it, but I woke up with my shirt drenched.

Priscilla and I squeezed two more dates out of each other. The last time, we were both mostly on our phones.

What can I say? It wasn't meant to be. Life, it chugs along.

• • •

Christmas season, Friday night at the mall. My old stomping grounds. The best time of the year, right? Yeah, yeah, yeah, shut your piehole.

I walk around and think, Nothing's changed. The gray tiles lifeless as ever, hella dirty, too, for bad measure. What used to be an Auntie Annie's is now space for rent. Waldenbooks is gone. People don't read anymore. They sure as hell don't go to the mall on Friday nights.

I stop right in front of the Dillard's, the one I used to work at, and stare up at the glowing white sign. All of a sudden, I'm getting kinda hungry.

I look down the walkway and see the woman in the distance with a toddler. She's holding the child's hand and they're moving in my direction. Moving closer. I watch closely—very, very closely.

Closer, closer, closer, then I process it's her. It's absolutely her.

Suddenly, a new organ seems to fatten in the space between my heart and my stomach. It's the size and density of a bowling ball, the motherfucker.

She bends down to tie the girl's shoes. Speaks something into her ear.

What immediately comes to my mind is, Who the Daddy be?

Then an urgent message from my command center:

Run.

Do it. Do it. Do it now.

I bolt across the lifeless tiles like idiot Forrest Gump, my braces fallen off. I hit my stride and I'm smiling. Why am I smiling? I'm disturbing the graveyard peace of the mall, the final resting place of yesteryear's capitalists. I don't look back. Not once do I look back. That's the important thing to remember here. I'm at the opposite end now. Sucking air. How sweet and painful the oxygen is. I realize how absurdly out of shape I am. I'm wheezing and wheezing and wheezing, and as I wheeze my stomach growls, then a hot stab pierces my right knee, the one I injured playing league basketball, and I grab my pathetic excuse for a knee as the pain spreads down my leg. My shirt is soaked in sweat and blood rushes to my head and my corpuscles deconstruct to goop. I'm losing weight now. I'm diving. Weightless. Wheeeeee!

. . .

A gentle tapping on my chinny-chin-chin helps me come to.

"He's alive!" shouts the little girl. "I knew he was playing dead, Mommy!"

From the ground, supine, I study the girl's face—not long enough to distinguish the similarities—then I turn toward her mother, who's kneeling beside her.

"Hey," I say.

"Hello," Columbia says. "Are you okay? Shall I call an ambulance?"

"Shall not," I answer. "I'm just resting my eyes. My bruised cortex."

Another sentence sprouts in my head and try as I might to repress it, it bum-rushes out of my throat like a convict on the run: "It's nice to know your phone's in working order."

She stares at me. Her eyes are the same, but not the same at all. For a hot second I can't read her but then her expression loosens into something that seems unreachably sad. Nostalgic. Before she can say another word, her daughter again taps my chin.

"Are you a monster, mister? Is your name Fwankenstein?"

. . .

"Hey, think you can be ready in fifteen minutes?" I ask my wife over the phone.

"What?"

"I'm going over to pick you up. I'm starvin' like Marvin."

"Aren't you out shopping right now?"

"Yeah, but I had a little accident and built up a healthy appetite."

"What? Did something happen?"

"Ran into a brick wall called My Past. I think I tweaked my knee."

"What?"

"Mall cops."

"Is everything okay?"

"Yeah. Everything's fine," I said.

"Why're you acting weird?"

"Usually, I always do."

"Look, I'm not ready right now. I need at least thirty more minutes."

"Thirty more minutes? All right, your wish is granted. How does IHOP sound?"

"IHOP?"

"Yeah. Been craving waffles and scrambled eggs. Maybe some pancakes too. Mmm, pancakes."

"Craving? You pregnant?"

"After last night, you might be," I said. "We might be."

"Shut up."

"All right. Be ready in thirty minutes?"

"You know, you're very annoying sometimes."

"I know. I usually always am."

"Ugh. Don't speed on the highway. Bye."

"Love ya too."

All the Pretty Paintings

∞

So we go to this gallery—me, Marie, the kids—and it's not only what I expect, it's worse. Awful, pointless, white. Everywhere white, the art and the crowd.

"Incredible," says Marie, in her signature monotone, swiveling her head left then right, which means she approves.

"Dumb," says Mikey, which means that in two minutes flat, he'll beg us to take him to GameStop.

"Wow," says Marie—I mean, Little Marie, or Mini-Me, I like to call her—swiveling her head left then right just like her mother, making the duo appear the girl version of Will Ferrell and Chris Kattan in *Night at the Roxbury*. You know the scene.

"Must be Mikey and me are the only two who don't get it," I say. With two women around constantly, I hesitate to make declarations. I prefer instead to pose perplexions. In the exchange of information with the fairer sex, the difference between declarations and perplexions is, I've learned, the difference between saying, for example, "You do look rather imposing in that dress, honey," and, "Honey, no, of course you look incredible, but haven't we both fallen off the fitness wagon?"

"Clearly, you don't understand nuance," says Mini-Me, raising her chin so high I spot a juicy little booger lodged in her nostril.

I smirk. "Nuance? What's nuance? Yo, Mikey, help me out here."

"I dunno," says my son curtly. "Can we please go to GameStop please? This place sucks!"

"Michael, language," I snap. "And no, we can't go to GameStop yet. We barely just got here. We have to appreciate all the pretty paintings."

Marie smiles at me tight-lipped and with eyes cold, black and hard like stones at the bottom of an old well. She squeezes my hand hard—hard enough—then ushers us, The Pack, toward the first canvas in sight.

Nothing's on it. Nothing at all. I mean, it's blank. Plain white pigment—*the conglomeration of all color*, says a snobbish voice inside my head. I don't know who this voice is, this phantom Pierre Escargot, but I sure do hate his stinking guts.

The first not-painting is by a Mexican artist called Fabricio.

Fabricio is standing next to his empty work, smiling tautly like Marie. He's tall with a bushy reddish beard.

"Simply amazing," says Marie, cupping her chin.

"Gracias," says Fabricio, bowing knightly to her. He registers the rest of The Pack, grin revealing a row of untrustworthy gold-capped front teeth.

"What was your general approach on this piece, señor?" Marie asks him, all polite.

"Pos, no-thing craycee," answers the slick Mexican, surrendering his hands to the air as if to proclaim, "It arrived to me as a gift from God, mi amor."

"Pos, I jus listened to mi corazon," he says to my wife.

"I can do *that*," blurts Mikey, furrowing his face at Fabricio's vacant canvas as if it had just squirted pickle juice on him.

"Be nice to the nice artist," I say to my son.

Fabricio bows, glances at me. "Gracias, señor."

The next not-painting is exactly like Fabricio's except smaller—much smaller, about half the size of a square of tissue.

"Now this," says Marie, monotonely. "Notice its diminutiveness. Small but aggressive. On the attack. I can feel it burrowing inside here," she says, tapping the center of her chest.

This little gem was manufactured by a Californian called Ken Nguyen, who's barely taller than my own Mikey.

"This is so stupid," says my son. "Can we pleasepleaseplease leave already?"

"Ohmygod, shut up about your stupid videogames," says Mini-Me.

"Mini-Me—Marie—not in front of the nice gentleman," I say.

"No worries," offers Ken Nguyen, bowing very Fabricio-like. What's with all these guys bowing like fancy British butlers? It makes me feel inappropriate, unbecoming, as if I'd shown up late with my family to the wrong birthday party.

"Believe you me, we really do appreciate your work," says Marie to Ken Nguyen. "The subject, the size, the composition—it belies man's true nature. A violence so pressurized, so intense, it's as dense as a skin-shearing neutron star."

"Flattered," says the pipsqueak painter, who's simultaneously—you guessed it—bowing.

The next not-painting, if one can even call it that, is an entire section of white wall upon which, smack on its center, is the name *Jamal Blackberry* written in black cursive no longer than a foot across.

"Behold," says the artist called Jamal in an accent I can't place, his branch-like arm stretched toward the wall, I mean, his mural.

"Incredible," says Marie. "The complete universe unto itself. Alpha and omega. The Word and Will of God, anchored by His Logos."

"Honored," says Jamal, bowing deeply but keeping his yellowy eyes glued to my wife.

"So, wouldn't it be like really cool if I did this?" blurts Mini-Me, whipping out a Sharpie then scribble-scratching lines across Jamal's John Hancock and replacing it with her own, dotting the "i" with a girly little heart.

Mikey laughs. Marie gasps. I swallow my spit.

Someone's cellphone hits the cement floor loudly and we're suddenly surrounded by a swarm of people, all white people—every one of them dressed in tweed jackets and pointing at us, The Pack, as though we're warty witches or no-good goblins who've invaded their mighty little castle.

"Shame!" a woman screams.

"Blasphemers!" a man hollers.

We're corralled and pushed and shoved and spun around—then just like that the chaos stops.

We're outside the gallery, where a light drizzle is falling, a cool breeze blowing.

We all look at each other, all of us stunned. Then, my family looks at me, and I shrug my shoulders. We walk back to our soccer-mom van in silence, all of us holding hands like a picture-perfect little unit.

On the way home, I finally break the silence.

"Well, that was fun, wasn't it?"

"Yeah," Mikey agrees. "Crowd-surfing was badass! I was basically like Drake!"

"You wish," says Mini-Me.

Marie glances at me, a warm matronly smile on her face.

After dinner—leftover spaghetti and meatballs—the kids go upstairs to get ready for bed and I help Marie with the dishes. I scrub a plate so meticulously it sparkles bright white under the kitchen light.

"Check it out," I say to her, holding the plate up high. "My masterpiece."

She examines the spotless ceramic, cupping her chin.

"It's missing something, hon—panache, maybe, or moxie. The special stuff. Keep chipping away at it, grasshopper."

Wearing a grin, she kisses me. Oh, she's a handful, my wife. She can be straight-up vicious like a deadly little cotton-mouth, but there's something about her that always tickles my toesies.

The next morning, after Marie leaves to drop off Mikey at batting practice, it's all over the local news. An installation by up-and-comer Jamal Blackberry sells for $1.3 million. The buyer, Chevy Chase Ford-Ferrari, a red-faced car dealership magnate, is shown chewing a fat Cuban cigar.

"Look!" I say to Mini-Me. "You're what the hoodlums call Instafamous!"

"Eww, like don't ever say 'hoodlums' again. And, ohmygod!"

My daughter and I land on discussing the finer points of copyright and intellectual property theft. Her knowledge amazes me and, after a while, I witness her face morph into a terrible older-looking mask I've never seen before, as if the thrill of her name appearing on television had expedited her entry into adulthood.

She asks out loud where her share of the pie is. Before my eyes, Little Marie, Mini-Me—my baby girl—threatens to call a lawyer.

"I'll take that rich prick to court for every penny he's worth if he thinks he can screw me over!" she yells.

"Marie, language," I say softly.

"You know what, I'm, like, gonna go to law school. Like, Harvard Law."

"Now sweetie," I say even softer, "we've plenty of time to plan your future. Let's take things one little step at a time, okay?"

"You know when I set my mind to doing something, *Daddy*,"

she says, meaty emphasis on my pet name, "I always see it through."

Mini-Me struts upstairs like a vengeful cat on the prowl—I don't know how else to describe it. It's something I've watched her mother do too many times before. Too many times to count.

The darndest thing is, I can't deny her claim: nothing fuels my baby girl more than good old-fashioned spite.

"You gonna take care of your momma and daddy when they're old and brittle?" I ask the stairway sans my daughter. Goodness, I think, my life's a Hallmark movie.

Out of curiosity—okay, and a teensy-weensy bit of dread—I pull out my phone and google Harvard Law tuition. What's the harm in knowing, right?

It spits back $65,875 a year.

Let me repeat that: $65,875 a year—$875 more than I make in an entire year.

I feel something hefty—dumbbell-like—slam down on my guts. I'm convinced it's the leftovers. Rotten old pasta.

"Exactly like her mother," I hear myself mutter, the hot residue of my words leaving my mouth sticky and fever-like.

Standing alone in my living room, the TV still on, I watch bands of sunlight breach through the white blinds and splash across my living room carpet. Every day, this happens without my consent. Then, for a few seconds, my cellphone buzzes on my sofa, also without my consent. Every day, at select times, I choose not to answer my calls. Then, for some reason—for no real good reason whatsoever, really—I bow. I bow to no one—except maybe to the wraiths I've always sensed loitering in my pantry, for I hold this truth to be self-evident that my house is haunted. And maybe to fathers and daughters and sons of noble mothers across the world. And to money in the bank and the bleeding spirit of America, that fickle bitch. And to decent health and hope that one day—someday—Jesus'll grant me the strength to pay off my mortgage on my two-story, four-bedroom cookie-cutter home of plain, white, ugly walls.

Coke Machine

∞

Milton Brown made his way to the far end of the mall, the side with the Sears with the busted sign that read *S ar*, and began his routine. He dunked his mop in the yellow bucket filled with murky water, twisted the handle.

Milton swung his mop in circles, producing large, glossy swirls on the dark tile. This was entertainment for him. He wasn't the type of man to bring an iPod to work. Not even a CD player. He believed he was too old for that shit.

After a while of swishing the mop around, imagining it as the girl he never took to the prom he never went to, Milton noticed a woman on her hands and knees by the Coke machine near the glass exit doors. She seemed to be looking for something, dropped money perhaps. From where he stood, Milton couldn't see her face—only a tangle of curly blonde hair. The mall wouldn't close for another two hours, but still, Milton wasn't used to seeing people on the far end this time of night.

"The hell's she up to?" Milton muttered.

He continued mopping, but kept glancing at the woman every few seconds. It seemed to Milton that she wasn't looking for something, but rather waiting. Waiting for something.

Overcome, Milton decided to approach her and find out. He walked to her slowly as not to startle her.

"Can I help ya with something, ma'am?" he asked. His voice seemed to echo in the empty mall.

The woman shot her head up at Milton. She was young, very young. There was a jagged pink scar on her cheek, and she wore a silver necklace with a small cross. A Christian. Milton thought he figured out the crazed look in her bloodshot blue eyes.

"There's a portal under here," the young woman said.

"A what-uh?"

"A portal. To the Pemberton vault with all the secrets. If I can get my hands on the recipes, I'll be rich. Super-rich!"

Milton scratched his balding head and wondered who the fuck Pemberton was, then he realized it didn't matter. This woman was whacked out, far gone, in another world. But Milton didn't judge these kinds of people. He understood their situation. That's because, long ago, Milton lost his only brother to drugs. His older brother, Troy, got mixed up with bad people, and eventually, got himself killed—a gunshot to the head. Blew all his brains out. That's how Milton remembered him.

For a good while, Milton too was mixed up in that world—a world he felt he had inherited. Like his older brother, he, too, once found himself on the business end of a gun, pointed right at his temple, all because he'd shortchanged a bad-tempered distributor named Keith ten dollars. As Milton was on his knees before Keith, hands locked behind his head execution-style, he thought about Troy, then closed his eyes and wept. Keith, seeing Milton weep like a little bitch, felt a surge of power spread through his body. This is what it feels like to be a god, Keith thought. I am a god. He loved the feeling of making a weak man get on his knees and beg for his life. Keith let Milton live, but said the next time he saw him, he'd better fucking have his hundred dollars ready, because that was the new price for his life. The next day, as Milton wandered the streets, feeling sick to his stomach, wondering how the hell he was going to scrounge up cash, he stumbled into a building where a nondenominational Christian service was taking place. Milton figured dropping in for a few minutes wouldn't hurt. He could use some uplifting. He stayed for the whole service. He was enthralled by Pastor James, who stood straight and talked straighter. After the service ended, Milton walked up to Pastor James and talked to him. Milton confessed everything, his life's problems and addictions. Pastor James, with calmness in his mien, listened without interrupting. When Milton finished, the pastor told him to hang on a minute, then walked off somewhere. When he returned, he held a hundred-dollar bill in front of Milton. He said, "Use this to get yourself out of trouble, son." Milton's knees trembled. He couldn't believe the pastor's kindness. All he'd wanted to do was talk. Milton felt like crying, getting on his knees again and crying. Instead, he accepted the Benjamin, stuffed it in his pocket, and asked, "Will you be here tomorrow?" Pastor James smiled and answered, "Yes," and, like that, Milton took a step toward freedom away from the bad world—a world that, as a minimum-wage janitor in a crumbling mall, felt vaguely familiar to him upon seeing the strange, drugged-up young blonde.

"I'm Milton," Milton said to the woman, bending down and extending his hand to her. At first, she stared at his hand like it was a knife, but then she understood the gesture and shook it.

"Wanna help me look for the portal?" the woman asked. "We'll split the money."

"Oh, that's okay, darling. I appreciate it," Milton replied, smiling faintly. He didn't know what else to say.

Milton recently read in the papers how a new drug from Florida called Clark Kent was sweeping across the nation. Kids were injecting the shit into their feet and, for a few hours, it made them feel invincible, like they could fly—like Superman. But then came the hallucinations, the cravings. Then death. The drug was killing them and killing them fast. Milton wondered if this young woman on the ground before him was on Clark Kent.

"Too bad so sad then," the woman said blandly. "More money for me."

"What's your name, darling?"

"Susannah."

Susannah lowered her head to the floor and resumed her search underneath the Coke machine.

"I'm gonna find it," she said, her voice directed under the machine. "Then I'm gonna be rich. Super-rich!"

There was no rhyme or reason for people in Susannah's condition, Milton thought. She was already gone.

"I know you will, darling, I know it." Milton got back on his feet.

The truth was, he wanted to help Susannah. Maybe it was her age, or the fact that she was a woman, or that he saw something of himself in her. Milton briefly considered offering to take her home for a hot meal and a warm bed so she could get right, but then he wondered how the hell that could work. It wasn't possible; it'd change up too many things. Plus, Milton didn't know Susannah at all, didn't know her history or the kinds of people she hung with. The idea of taking in a complete stranger in this day and age was straight-up crazy. Perhaps, if Milton was younger, a "young buck," as Pastor James had called him, he'd've thought otherwise, but now he had to think about himself. The rest of his life, an older man.

Milton walked away from Susannah, as slowly as he came.

The next four days, as Milton made his way to the far end of the mall, he saw Susannah by the Coke machine, peeking underneath it, searching for her portal. She became part of his routine landscape. Somehow, seeing her comforted him.

On the third day, Milton called out to Susannah.

"Still looking, darling?"

"I'm gonna find it, you'll see," Susannah answered. "Then I'm gonna be rich. Super-rich!"

"I know you will, darling, you'll find it."

On day five, Milton decided, What the hell? He'd join Susannah in her search. He'd get on all fours, even if just for a few minutes, help out. It wouldn't hurt, and, sometimes it's beneficial to change things up.

When Milton got to the far end of the mall, he found that Susannah wasn't there. This deflated him. The sensation was like arriving at the movie theater only to find out the movie you were dying to see is sold out. Still, during his mopping, Milton couldn't help but glance at the Coke machine every now and then. Foolishly, he hoped, like a child, that Susannah would materialize.

The next night, when Milton saw that Susannah was still gone, worry set in. Perhaps she was in some alley, on the ground in the fetal position by a dumpster, a needle stuck in her heel. Milton didn't want to think about that, but he couldn't help it. He quickly became angry with himself. This showed in his work as he pushed the mop around roughly. He was ashamed. He pondered all the things he could've said and all the things he could've done. After everything Pastor James had done for him, this was how he returned the favor? Fucking asshole, thought Milton of himself. Motherfucking selfish asshole.

Later, calmed down, Milton wondered what it was that made people better versions of themselves in their heads. This was a question that had no right or wrong answers.

The next day, his day off, Milton decided to do something he hadn't done in seven years as a mall janitor: go to the mall.

He made his way to the far end and his heart pumped like crazy.

The night before, Milton had had a dream that Troy took him to shoot hoops at Miller Park. Troy commanded, all serious, "Let's roll," then he jumped and flew off like a crow. As a crow. Milton stood stunned on the court. He stared at the gray sky and accepted the absurdity of it all. When he woke up, Milton hopped out of bed and splashed cold water on his face. Unsettled, he thought of the dream as an omen. Pastor James had convinced him long ago that all dreams, one way or another, were omens. Visions from God, or Hell.

When Milton approached the red glow—the Coke machine—and no Susannah, his anxiety flushed out of him in an ugly way.

"Goddamn waste of time," he muttered. "Omens my ass."

Milton looked at the busted Sears sign. Now that he was here, he thought about walking inside the store. But there wasn't a damn thing he wanted to buy. He felt out of place all of a sudden, and now all he wanted to do was get the hell out of Dodge.

His stomach growled.

He hadn't eaten anything all day. His headspace made sense, knowing his mood was tied to his eating. Before he left, Milton decided to grab pretzel bites and a soda.

Staring at the Coke machine, Milton couldn't recall the last time he'd bought a soda from a machine.

He spotted something shiny on the ground near the machine. He bent down and picked up a silver necklace with a small cross. Susannah's, or one just like hers. Milton wondered if she was aware she'd dropped it, but then realized that was a ridiculous thing to think.

Crouched, Milton then got on all fours and lowered his face to the floor. The tile was cold against his cheek. He knew he was acting impulsive, a little nuts, but he couldn't care less. Nobody was at the mall.

Under the Coke machine was nothing. Just dust and darkness. Milton wondered, What does a portal look like anyway? Big or small? Do they make loud noises or are they as silent as cemeteries? Do they have blue energy rings around them or are they invisible? Where do they lead to—worlds with purple skies and red oceans and little green men, or inside huge vaults filled with gold bars and secret recipes?

As Milton stared into the darkness, he heard the hum of the machine. It was a sound he'd never really listened to before. It could put him to sleep if he listened long enough.

A short while later, Milton got back on his feet. His knees and lower back were achy. Still clasping the silver cross necklace, which felt sweaty in his hands, he stuffed it inside his pocket.

He left the mall and on the walk back to his truck, he thought, You're too old for this shit. Too fucking old.

On the drive home, Milton couldn't quite put his finger on it, but he felt as if something small but important, like an old lever, had been cranked inside him in the opposite direction. He was on edge. He smacked his lips and tasted metal, bitterness. His tongue was bone-dry. He'd forgotten to get food. All that stupid shit about portals had made him forget. His stomach growled again, and the only thing Milton could do was groan. He squeezed his old leathery steering wheel until veins emerged on the top of his hands like wild, black tentacles.

City Lights From
the Upside Down

∞

Walking into work, I munched on a Quaker Chewy Chocolate Chip Granola Bar, swigged the last drops of hot Aquafina water that'd boiled overnight in my car.

San Antonio, July 2010. Hell's kitchen sink. Not a nice place for a white Mexican't like me. For anybody with epidermis, really.

Walking into work, I remember thinking, I'll be in Boston this time next year sipping hot chocolate.

Dragging my feet through the glass door with a huge blue "N" embossed on it, I remember thinking, When the fuck're you gonna actually apply to grad school?

Cora, my insurance training buddy for three months—beautiful Cora, her heart-shaped face I won't soon forget—smiled at me as I passed her in the breakroom. She too was twenty-one but was three years behind in college—she'd had a kid. Baby-daddy problems, as the kids said.

In those days I worked in a call center because, because ...

Look, how could I know then just how badly my private loans would rip my ass up later on? Absorbed in the present, at the time, it was as if the future awaited me like a salaried paycheck. My name ink-dried and saved in the servers.

The things they never tell you: the berserk nature of thoughts that flit across your mind in a stuffed cubicle; the brain-fry of buzzing fluorescent office lights; the rigid impracticality of Payless dress shoes bending your aching arches; the advent of Murphy's Law and the foibles of fallible insurance policies. Me, I kept busy, chewed my fingernails to bloody stubs. Lived in the present and such.

"When're you off today?" whispered Enrique, who I could hear but not see. We were siloed, him and I, by a gray wall divider—two softcore cell inmates.

"What time do you show?" I said.

"Say again?"

"Hey," I said, "wanna grab lunch today? There's that little mom-and-pop Thai joint down the road. To be honest, I'm sick and tired of Wendy's."

"Sorry bro," Enrique said, "already ate. It's like three o'clock, dude."

We never did go out to lunch, Enrique and me. I recall his spectacled face, large and folded, caramel like desert sand. I could be mixing him up with someone else. That's very possible. It's getting harder and harder to tell.

In addition to my fingers, I constantly chewed Big Red gum. I'd always been hyperaware of my breath, even when talking to client-strangers on the phone. Remember, this was before I began to regularly floss. There existed, somewhere, a company policy about not chewing gum while on the job. However, when young, brash and a self-proclaimed Marxist as I was—in my daydreams, at least—the rules slide off you like rain.

Speaking of torrential storms, one day I got soaked on my walk into work. I was a twenty-one-year-old guy, therefore had found it useless to own my own umbrella. No umbrella and coached in insurance—there's a first-rate joke there I'll write down someday. I left home before long, didn't wait to catch cold from the downstream blast of air-conditioning directly above my desk, didn't alert my supervisor.

"No more funny business," he warned me the next day. It was only because he'd known my older cousin in high school—they'd played varsity basketball together—that he didn't fire me on the spot.

I nodded and he nodded back; we fist-bumped. He must've really believed he was doing me a solid. "Funny business." Who did he think I was, Kermit the Frog?

If you want to force your discovery of poetry—and I mean in

an exceptionally exceptional way—follow after me: answer the endless phone calls, lose track of them even if The Man doesn't, even if just for a short while. If you're interested, I'll send you the link to apply, though it's been over a decade since I've set foot inside that old brick building. I know I'll never do so again.

Here's how I eventually came to imagine the downtown San Antonio skyline: jagged row of bottom teeth meets toothless blue chasm. As in, so wide open how else does 9/11 happen? As in, so wide open how else can birds fly? The sun, erstwhile—supreme Marxist—bakes us, his restless comrades, his faithful sons and daughters.

I should mention now that I took Cora out on two dates—both times to Mi Tierra on a Friday evening after work—after which the second date we mutually decided, without using our words, that things weren't going to work out between us. That's how I remember it, at least. It's very likely it shook out that way. It's getting harder and harder to tell. After our second outing we hugged goodbye—she smelled great—and later I'd rationalize that if I was the universe and the universe was me, I was nearly fourteen billion years old and my collision with Cora was nearly fourteen billion years in the making, and the sad truth is the payoff doesn't match the anticipation, not by a long shot.

One day while in the office, the sour aftertaste of mustard and dill pickle relish haunting my tongue, I took a call and assisted a lienholder. Exactly as written, easy as pie. To memory, it's the smoothest call I've ever been paid to answer. At the end of our brief transaction, the lienholder expressed satisfaction at my "superb" customer service. I replied to him, "Happy Fourth of July!" After which I immediately realized my embarrassing mistake, then amended myself, "Happy fifth of July!"

Enrique laughed so loud our gray wall divider juddered, knocking down the only adornment I'd tacked up on my side—a polaroid of our soon-to-be deceased family Golden Retriever, Attaboy—which landed in my trash bin.

"Happy fifth of July," Enrique repeated, "man, that's some original shit right there. Where do you come up with this material?"

"I got it from my momma," I replied stoically, thinking of the song by will.i.am.

Enrique informed me he'd worked in insurance for eight years.

"Eight long years," he added.

"Eight years sure is a long-ass time," was all I managed to say back to him before I hopped on another call.

I should also mention that that summer, which launched the beginning of a two-year citywide drought, that for maybe two or three weeks a bright light not-quite star and not-quite angel followed me home at night. Wherever I'd fixed my gaze, so too there it was. I made the error of mentioning it to Cora on our second-and-last rendezvous and, judging from the expression in her swollen eyes, I knew she believed me to be another magical thinker. A man of myth and fiction, too untethered from her gritty realm of baby-daddies. I was not yet a father—I couldn't understand—and consequently I was on the other side. I asked to see another photo of her daughter; she said her phone had died.

O the ferocious irony of meter and rhyme.

It was only later, much later, when I immortalized that unforgettable alien presence in a poetry collection I had published last year, my first book, titled: *City Lights From the Upside Down*. My publisher in Los Angeles had recommended I consider "Downside Up" instead of "Upside Down," pointing out that some readers, especially younger ones, may anticipate a connection to the hit Netflix show, *Stranger Things*. I wrote him back in an email: "I've never watched the show. Plus, *City Lights From the Downside Up* implies normal field vision—nothing too extraordinary, no? Although," I'd concluded in mock e-humility, "I'm not at all suggesting my book will be extraordinary. Not at all."

To date, I've sold 199 copies, performed five readings at used bookstores and public library basements—but really, who's counting?

I'm serious, that wasn't a rhetorical question. I ask again: who's really keeping the score?

Men Without Hearts, Inc.

∞

They say when you fall in love, you give her a piece of your heart. So when things go bad, and she's gone, you lose a piece of yourself—forever.

I agree with all that except I never *gave* Luz a piece of my heart; no, she *took* it, pillaged the whole beating bleeding thing like a Viqueen. Well, I let her.

My punishment for leaving my chest wide open is living without a heart.

Outside, it's getting dark, raining heavily. The golden hour's fading. The lights are on upstairs, and I'm upstairs sitting on my father's favorite rocking chair. Rocking.

Don't ask if I'm home. The worst question is the kind whose answer is obvious. A purloined letter kind of question.

· · ·

When I got a letter in the mail, an invitation/application to join Men Without Hearts, Inc., I was eager to sign up, send them their requested $250 annual club fee. Basically, all the money I had to my name.

If you'll recall, Biggie Smalls once said, "Mo' money, mo' problems." My motto has always been, "No money, no problems!"

The invitation said in two to three months, after payment is received, the club would ship me a piece of some poor sap's chemically treated heart in the form of a pill—a little chewable—so I could feel something, anything, again.

Hooray.

Until then, I had to wander Earth without a core.

Without a ticker to match the rhythm of my footsteps, or at the very least provide me a beat to tap my foot to, time was relative, irrelevant—yesterday's newspaper in the hands of an actuary.

In other words, I had all the time in the world, and nowhere to dump it.

• • •

I miss her body, the way she filled out her Levi's, the way she let me slide my hands under her blouse, run my greedy fingers up and down her dark curves, lick her salty-sweet Luz skin, give her goosebumps.

I miss her mind, that shadowy jungle, the way Luz chuckled at kids in restaurants choking on food—naughty girl—and the way she got dead-serious gazing at lonely old men in diners shuffle off to the restroom. "Their time's up, baby, and ours has just beguneth," I'd tell her in these saturated situations. She'd look at me with slitted eyes, blazing lips, and respond with something to the tune of, "You talk like an amateur hedonist, honey, a boy who's yet to grow into his own fur." My arms and legs were only mildly hairy.

I had to admit: the girl was deep.

I miss her farts, silent but deadly, always while I drove, always her devilish grin a sign of her Catholic guilty conscience.

I miss her smile, her straight white teeth—her long thin neck I could wrap my hands around gently.

I miss being, at her allowance, my own pseudomythical creation: King of her Mind, Body & Soul. I miss my one true Viqueen.

Luz.

. . .

It's been four months and still no package. I'm obsessed with waiting for the mail. I can tell that Daryl, my postman, is frightened to death of me. He probably wishes I were dead. Some days I think I am. It could be my breath. Brushing my teeth again, flossing, might help my case. Listerine strips, too, if I could afford them.

It could also be the gaping hole in my chest, the very wound Daryl was transfixed by.

"This?" I said, thumbing to it. "This is just a significant chasm in my center. An empty tomb. You can poke it if you want. It doesn't really hurt anymore."

"You craycee, mayne, you craycee," Daryl said, taking a step backwards.

"Why Dare-Dare," I said, stepping toward him, reaching out to pat his shoulder.

"Don't you touch me, craycee mayne!"

Yet my palm had already found its desired destination.

. . .

Five months.

I've been ripped off. Scammed. There's no magical capsule coming. I'm a victim of my own problems—of hoaxes, schemes, conspiracies and pilfered adoration.

I must wander this world without a core. Deserving punishment.

Ever heard of Hammurabi's Code? Universal law? Karmic justice? Cosmic indifference? Chaos theory?

Yeah, yeah, yeah. Hate to break it to you, sweetie, but those're just fancy labels for "Tough fucking luck."

Six months.

Wandering.

Broke.

Broke and heartless. Heartless and broke—don't know which combination sounds doper.

My beard is big and poofy. My body's skinny, twig-like, stinks something awful too, according to the masses.

What's my age again? I don't remember. It's easier to forget than you might think.

What's there left to register?

Aha, registers! Ka-ching.

I could have all the money and jewels in the world, but still no core. No girl.

Cold. I'm very cold. Brrr.

Did I mention it barely stopped raining this morning?

Today, I met some kids at the park. They stared at my chest, seemed impressionable enough.

"There's nothing there for you to see, children, so look into my orbs!" I shouted. "Here's your lesson for today: When heartless, hold on tight to your money!"

They made like sissy bananas and split.

Me, I stayed put, looked up at the sky, spotted the sun peeking out of the clouds finally.

"Hey there, Mr. Sol," I announced. "It's good to see you, been a while."

Then it hit me: Talking warmed me up, replaced stagnant vapors in my body with a fresh breeze as though the ocean was around the corner. It was exactly what the underground doctor had ordered, and it felt incredible—felt incredible to feel incredible!

Now I just needed to recalibrate my inside-voice. Tackle one problem at a time. Yeah. That was plenty of work to keep a mere mortal busy.

If I Drown, Play
Some Bill Withers
for Me

∞

All we'd talked about all week was pigging out on Subway pizza. Bump their watery, five-dollar footlongs—and Jailbird Jared, too—but their pizzas, though! Chef's kiss.

Sally was still in workshop. I waited for her in the bar at Chili's. I was pooped after an arduous day of teaching multiplication to booger-lickers. One day, I thought, they'll appreciate my instruction. But by then, I'd probably be sucking oxygen tanks dry.

I ordered a glass of water, considered tipping the bartender a buck, didn't. Some things in life are free.

A couple sips later, Sally texted me she was out. I drove to the Subway near her condo, the one next to a taco truck managed by Indians-from-India who said to each passerby, "hola, howdy." I'd offered to pick her up, but she wanted to meet me there.

In the parking lot, her face glowed in the streetlight like a Rembrandt—large, downturned almond eyes, vague. Even after another Earth rotation, gravity's constant drag, I realized again, looking at Sally, her ring finger, how damn lucky I was. Damn-lucky boy, me.

She let me kiss her lips as she stood statue-still. It was like smooching with a mannequin, except the most exotic mannequin sheathed in piquant, pliant skin. We were both exhausted, I figured.

I ordered a pepperoni pizza with jalapenos, extra mozzarella, a pinch of oregano and half a bag of Cool Ranch Doritos on top. The sandwich artist said, "You're one bad motherfucker."

"Damn straight," I agreed.

Sally ordered the same thing minus the chips but added tuna and onions. So not the same thing at all.

"Is that too much?" she asked me.

"Pepperoni, tuna and onions—sounds scrumptious!" I fibbed.

She grabbed a bag of Hot Cheetos off the rack, but I gave her side-eye, so she put them back.

As we waited for our pizzas to finish baking, the sandwich artist jammed out to something loud playing from his wireless Beats. Had he worn them the whole time we were there? I heard what I thought sounded like Ice Cube, but it could've very well have been Ice-T or Vanilla Ice.

After I paid, Sally sat us in a corner table near the restrooms. She liked being in corners to "keep an eye on folks." Her dad was a cop, so her hypervigilance didn't fall far from the handcuffs.

"I'm so hangry it ain't even funny," she said.

"Chow time," I proclaimed.

My pizza was gone in two minutes flat. I ate like a tiger shark around a shipwrecked crew.

"What'd I tell you about chewing your food slowly," Sally lectured.

"Uh-huh," I mumbled.

A couple years prior, I'd almost choked to death on a curly fry at a burger joint. Sally had to karate-chop my back a hundred times and at every chop she'd screamed, "HI-YA!" After I coughed up the fry the whole restaurant cheered, and Sally was mad at me for two days back to back. (Pun intended.) She didn't particularly take to me calling her Sally Bruce Lee Jet Li Chan after the incident. (Not to mention Sally Field before it, even though we both agreed Sally Field is a great American actress.) Sally swiftly introduced her Ten-Chews-A-Bite Rule, to which I violated during every meal thereafter. Good times.

She left half her pizza uneaten, looked queasy.

"You all right?" I asked.

"I think I'm sick."

"You do look a little sick."

"I feel like crap."

"You do look a little crappay."

"Let's go."

"Leggo my eggo," I said, and we left.

Outside, I hugged her tight, sniffed her hair—shampooey with a tinge of musk. I was about to kiss her lips again but she turned away, so I settled for cheek-peck. She was all clammed up. Mannequin-like.

"No more pizzas ever again," she said all serious.

"You said that last month."

"Yes. But I mean no more, ever again."

"Oh, okay. Ever again as in ...?"

"As in we're done."

"Oh, okay. We're done as in ...?"

"As in I can't fucking do this anymore. I just can't. I'm sorry."

She handed me her promise ring—$150 at Zales. Not on sale.

"What's this?" I said.

I went in for another kiss but she pushed me away.

"Stop that! You always mitigate pain with fantasies like everything's okay, but everything's not okay, don't you understand? Everything's not okay!"

"Sally, we talked about this already. C'mere, come to Papa."

Crying, she got inside her car and started the engine. Uh oh. I approached it and placed my hand on the driver's window.

"What about Paco?" I asked both her and my dashing reflection. Paco was our loveable pet iguana, who'd been moving slower and slower in those days.

She sped off, her tires screeching. It was so climactic I was panging Buncha Crunch—my go-to candy at the movie theater. Okay, that was a bad dad joke delivered in poor taste.

I felt strange eyeballs on me and turned around and saw the sandwich artist outside, posted up against the Subway entrance, smoking a cigarette, Beats headphones still on.

"Your girl just dump you, huh? Damn, dude. That's some messed-up shit, and I've seen lots of messed-up shit during my time here."

"Had it coming," I said.

What he said next is the spiritual climax of this depraved story, a moment which nearly drew from my eyes scant tears.

"Would you like a couple cookies for the road? They're on me. I gotchu, my guy."

I studied my fellow man for a few seconds, dumbfounded in admiration.

"You, sir, are a gentleman and a scholar and, above all, a sandwich virtuoso—I didn't catch your name."

"Harrison," he said.

"I appreciate your generosity, Harrison," I said, and then I walked to my truck, my head held high.

On my drive home, "Ain't No Sunshine" played on the radio. Bill Withers' serenade soaked me in alien misery. Somehow, it was beautiful. No—*therefore*, it was beautiful.

The road was dark and empty. The planet had always been that way, but I was only just seeing it. To quote Kurt Vonnegut, my peepholes were only just opening.

I zipped past so many green lights—escaped them—which is to say, I attempted busting out of my gorilla brain.

Time was inscrutable. It was like watching beach sand being blown endlessly by warm, coastal winds. Or observing legions of earthworms slide across thick mud.

I drove past a boy, I think, sitting on the edge of a wooden pier. He seemed to be gazing into the muck that was the Gulf of Mexico. The full moon reflected brightly off the filthy ocean's surface, where underneath, I knew, were sea creatures lurking, grinning dementedly.

I grabbed the bottle of Jack underneath my seat, popped it open and swigged from it, pirate-like.

Ahhh. Shiver me timbers.

That's how one made up for tragedy. By doing the sensible thing, which is to say, doing the thing that's right in front of you.

I recall only the loud, metal explosion. Everything else is subject to change.

I'd aimed for a watery grave—Davey Jones' Locker—but had to settle instead for a soft hospital bed

. . .

The pretty, blonde nurse instructed me to try my hand at poetry, so I came up with this:

Gunshot between the eyes,

Instantaneous demise.

"Wow!" Nurse Tiffany said. "Vivid imagery! You're a natural!"

"I get it from my mother," I said. "What's your last name?"

"Blanco. I'm like, half Spanish, or Portuguese, or whatever."

Other than banging Tiffany after I recovered, I don't remember much after my hospital days. Daze. Get it?

Tiff. A big ol' freak, that one. She was twice divorced, which perhaps factored into why that fake Spanish sorceress turned me onto crack. Yes—exactly the kind you're thinking of.

Since then, it's been one white vaporous tail after another. I slither across space, track strangers, stare at them, make them squirm. Then I laugh. Ah-ah-ah-ah-ah-ah-ahhhhhh.

Sometimes I like to think my smirk speaks for itself. Sometimes I like to think it boasts, in an iconic James Earl Jones baritone: *We'll end up in the same place, you and I. Ready or not.*

The Sad Tale of the
Inflatable Wacky
Tube Man

∞

Wheeler peeked out the window blinds and watched a police cruiser pull into his car lot. Two male officers stepped out, one short, the other tall. Tall Guy marched up the concrete walkway leading to the small wooden administrative building of Wheeler's Wheels-n-Deals. Wheeler gulped. He noticed Shorty moving toward the signpost, where there was mounted a stringy green Inflatable Wacky Tube Man, flapping about in fine form this midsummer—rather flippantly, if you asked Shorty.

Wheeler stepped outside to intercept Tall Guy.

"Hello, sir," the officer greeted. "You the owner of this business?"

"Yes I am, officer," Wheeler answered cautiously. He offered his hand. "Ted Wheeler. How can I help you?"

"Mr. Wheeler, um, uh, I don't quite know how to put this lightly." The officer scratched the back of his head. "I'll just cut to it. We have orders from the city to remove that thing from your property. Effective immediately." He pointed toward the Inflatable Wacky Tube Man. "We've received numerous complaints of assault."

From the city? Wheeler thought, as if he hadn't heard the part about assault.

Wheeler read the officer's shiny golden nametag: J. Christiansen.

Officious little prick, thought Wheeler. He'd read that in *The Shining* and never forgot it. It was a good line he kept in his back pocket, just in case, though he'd never actually used it. When Wheeler met a person he disliked, which in his shady line of work was every single day, he repeated that line in his head like clockwork.

"I don't think I understand, Officer Christiansen," Wheeler said, trying to control his rising temper. "What'd you mean by orders from the city?"

Christiansen lifted his duty belt authoritatively. Another whiner, he thought.

"Sir," Christiansen said firmly, straightening his back to make the most of his six-foot-four frame, "we've received approximately ten reports from individuals—eight women and two young men—who've been assaulted by that thing." He pointed again toward the Inflatable Wacky Tube Man, who, as always, was flapping and grinning. "The reports are all similar in nature. The victims claimed as they were leaving this premises, they were assaulted by that thing. Touched inappropriately. I won't get into details, but we don't play around with that. The city's cracking down, so I have my orders."

Wheeler looked behind Christiansen and saw Shorty crouched next to the Inflatable Wacky Tube Man, whose only crime, Wheeler now believed, was he hadn't drummed up enough business, though his dead wife who'd bought it for him as a birthday present two years ago had promised otherwise. From Wheeler's perspective, it appeared as though Shorty was trying to shut down the Inflatable Wacky Tube Man.

Wheeler's blood boiled.

"Hey, what's your partner doing over there?" Wheeler said angrily. "Hey asshole, take a hike! That's private property!"

"Sir," said Christiansen, irritated, his right hand now instinctively on his gun, "we're gonna take him away. End of discussion. Sexual assault is a serious crime. Unless you wanna be arrested for interference, I suggest you calm down."

Shorty, who also had a short fuse, couldn't find the switch to turn off the Inflatable Wacky Tube Man. This angered him. He looked up at the Inflatable Wacky Tube Man and suddenly, it seemed as if he was being mocked by that ridiculously predatory grin. Shorty snapped open his large pocketknife and slashed at the Inflatable Wacky Tube Man's base over and over. He savaged it, ripped open the fabric wholly.

"Not so funny anymore, are ya?" Shorty said to his defenseless and deflating victim.

Just before the Inflatable Wacky Tube Man flattened to the pavement, by some twisted miracle beyond the laws of logic, by a final act of resistance against brutality, by just a perfectly timed gust of strong midsummer wind, he swooped down and smacked Shorty right on his buttocks, hard. Shorty hopped and hollered like Yosemite Sam. He wore cowboy boots and an orange mustache, like Yosemite Sam.

"Damn thing got my ass!" he screamed.

Christiansen, having witnessed the whole thing, chuckled.

"My partner's a bit of a drama queen as you can see."

Christiansen then realized he wasn't chatting with one of his buddies. Everyday absurdities had a way of taking him out of his element.

He saw that Wheeler was on the ground, on his knees, hands covering his face. Sobbing.

"Uh, sir."

"My wife ... my only friend," Wheeler cried.

Wheeler was in shambles—a sad sight of a grown man to behold.

"Good God," Christiansen muttered, scratching the back of his head. "Good God."

"Goddang!" Shorty exclaimed in the distance, huge smile across his face. "We got ourselves a big one. A fighter!"

The Inflatable Wacky Tube Man wasn't a fighter anymore. He was simply no more. He'd been reduced to just a long piece of shredded green fabric dragged unceremoniously against concrete by a feisty little police officer with a Napoleon complex. He'd be placed in a cardboard box as criminal and evidence. By next week, he'd be forgotten.

Long Time No See

∞

I sip morning coffee at a Starbucks I'm at every Saturday and pretend to read The New York Times. I skim headlines, wonder how wonderful it'd be if I actually read the articles.

I look up and see Bob. I haven't seen Bob in three years, not since I left my last job. I'm not thrilled to see him, but not unhappy either. He told corny jokes and had a fittingly vanilla, somewhat unlikable face. You could say once upon a time, I invested a few stock-shares in Bob's life.

I wave at Bob. Bob, in line, sees me and squints, then smiles and waves back. After he gets his drink, he walks over to me and shakes my hand, then sits down at my table, real formal.

"Bobby boy," I say. "Long time no see."

"What's going on with you, Porridge Breath? Never see you around here."

"I'm always here," I counter. "Bob, you look exactly the same. As handsome and dickless as a G.I. Joe."

"Correction," Bob says, "they still call me Stretch Armstrong."

Bob flits his eyes down south and waggles his near-invisible eyebrows. Nobody ever called him Stretch Armstrong.

"Your mother would know more about that," I say.

We laugh. I sip my coffee and Bob slurps his light green sludge.

"What're you having?" I ask.

"Oh, you know, just a … … … …."

Bob strings together a series of words the sum of which loses me entirely. I don't know why I even asked him the question. I couldn't care less.

"Cool," I say coolly.

"And you? What're you having?" Bob asks.

"Coffee," I answer. "Plain black coffee. See, Bob, I keep it simple. Only takes me three words."

My tone comes off strong, but luckily for me, Bob hasn't a clue about social cues.

"You always were a routine guy," Bob says, a twinkle in his lazy gray eye. "Does your mom still make you tamales? Man, I never forget the time she brought some in. They were muy yum-yum!"

"Nope," I say to Bob. "No more yummy tamales." I have no idea why I lie.

Bored, I change the subject.

"So how's Joanie?" I ask.

"Joanie," Bob says, taking a quick breath. "Well, her and I divorced three years ago."

"Jesus," I say. "I'm sorry. I—I didn't know."

"Of course you didn't know," Bob says. "How would you?"

"You're right," I say.

I sip my coffee and Bob slurps his green stew.

"And Mitchell?" I ask. "How's that rascal doing?"

"Mitchell," Bob says, taking a deeper breath. "Well, the thing about Mitchell is Joanie took him. I haven't seen him in a while. I miss him. I sure do miss him a lot."

"Jesus, Mary and Joseph," I say. "I'm sorry, Bob. I'm firing blanks, aren't I?"

"It's okay," Bob says. "You didn't know."

"You're right, I didn't," I say.

I sip my coffee and Bob slurps his booger mush. Watching and hearing him do so is nauseating. Exhausting.

"And Clara and Abe?" I ask. "Did they end up getting hitched after all?"

Bob wipes his lips, sighs, and then says, "They did, but they're dead now."

I almost spit out my coffee in Bob's face.

"Christ!" I say. "They're *dead?*"

"Yes," Bob says plainly. "They died in a car accident in Vermont. Abe smashed into a bus head-on. He was going eighty. Him and Clara died instantly. Happened in broad daylight. They guessed Abe was texting and driving. He wasn't much of a drinker."

"Good God," I say. "Vermont? How does something like that happen in Vermont?"

"The lesson here," Bob says as though he's a preacher, "is that death isn't restricted to any one geographic location. It happens anywhere, even in Vermont."

I feel something heavy inside roll around. It wasn't there when I first got to Starbucks.

"And Nate?" I venture to ask, hopeful I'll receive some good news for a change. "Please tell me your brother's doing all right?"

Bob stares at me for a few seconds, silent, then smiles. Phew! I think. I finally hit a shot.

Bob shakes his head side to side.

"Dead," he answers. "We lost Nate last Christmas. After his gastric-bypass surgery, he stopped eating. He lost almost two hundred pounds and got real sick. My mom went into depression."

All I manage to do is to sip a long, slow sip of coffee, now lukewarm.

Bob slurps his liquid diarrhea, in turn churning my stomach. I want—or so I believe—to sprinkle upon him the surplus benevolence in my reserves, but he's rendering that spiritually impracticable.

"Can you please stop doing that?" I snap.

Bob looks at me with his vanilla face—a face so stupid and garish I wonder why I even decided to engage with it.

I glance at his hand and notice a silver wedding ring. Was his old one gold? He'd mentioned his divorce with Joanie, but I desperately need to hear something positive—who his new wife is.

"Bobby boy," I say, nodding toward his ring, "at least you caught yourself another one. To tell you the truth, I wasn't a big fan of Joanie. She was argumentative and full of herself. She thought she looked like Joan Crawford, but really, she looked like a retarded wallaby. So what's the lucky new lady's name?"

Bob looks at his ring and smiles.

"I'm not remarried," he answers. "I just couldn't bring myself to take this off."

I'm off the reservation now. Going eighty, ninety, a hundred. Looking for something, anything, to smash into.

"You insufferable buffoon!" I shout. "You're fucking relentless, Bob, as fucking relentless as King Harod in a children's hospital!"

Bob stares at me for a moment, silent, then giggles. He giggles loud, his eyes closed like he's a gigantic baby. Other patrons stare at us.

Suddenly, something inside me softens, and I laugh too. I can't help it. I laugh along with Bob. Bob giggles and I laugh.

After a while, Bob finally says, "Good one, Pete. Good one. Man, I haven't heard King Harod's name in a long time. You're a riot, Pete, a real riot!"

Bob giggles again, and this time the patrons join him. They all lose their minds.

I sip my coffee and feel the cold joe bubble in my guts. I feel the weight of death lift off my shoulders. Aliveness, I think, what a tremendous thing while it lasts.

Amidst Bob and the roaring audience, I stand and raise my arms to the roof, to heaven and hell beyond it.

"Bob," I proclaim, my hands clenched into fists, "I'm going to stab your stupid fucking body until your stupid fucking intestines fall out, then I'm going to feast on them and shit on your stupid fucking mother's stupid fucking grave!"

Bob and the crowd explode as though I just told the greatest joke in the world. They laugh so hard they fall out of their chairs and writhe in pain on the dirty floor, all the while pointing at me. Everyone pointing at me.

I'm standing, the only one upright, the only one quiet. I try to hear myself think, but can't. I'm drowned out.

When the laughter dies down soon—hopefully soon, I pray—I'll ask the barista for a plastic knife.

The Savage
Screwball

∞

I was at Starbucks sipping coffee, reading Roberto Bolaño's *The Savage Detectives*, when a feeling hit me: Everything was perfect.

The sensation was so striking I put the book down.

I looked outside: the sun was smiling, birds chirped, traffic advanced smoothly. The world was a mid-century postcard.

Emboldened, feeling especially good after my morning workout, I texted Vanessa if she could come over tomorrow night. I said I could cook lasagna and buy a bottle of red wine, her favorite.

"Here ya go," said Madeline, the tall, beautiful barista with bright tattoo sleeves, placing a fresh-out-of-the-oven chocolate chip muffin in front of me. The waft of baked dough was delectable.

"Thank you. They don't pay you enough," I flirted.

"But I get to see that smile of yours," she flirted back.

Oh Madeline. I imagined us spending a day at the beach, me admiring her resplendent body art when I heard a bang. A man had pushed open the door into Starbucks. He had dark skin, army fatigue pants, crazed homeless eyes. He stunk. He looked to be my dad's age. He peered left, right, straight ahead, then spotted me. He marched right up to me.

"Hey, let me bum a few bucks, dude," he said. He smelled like a dead animal. His face was like expired beef jerky.

I patted my pocketless basketball shorts—my wallet was on the table—and said:

"Sorry, sir. Don't carry cash."

The man's face twisted in ugly directions—was plain ugly.

"Little prick," he mumbled, then marched right out of Starbucks.

Despite the insult, what struck me most was that he was clean-shaven. Some things don't add up only after you think about them.

I felt someone's eyes pierce the back of my head, so I turned around and caught an old black woman shaking her permed head at me.

"Yes?" I said.

She swiftly lifted up her Vanity Fair magazine to cover her face, effectively blocking me out.

I see how it is, I thought. Then my phone buzzed. Mom.

"Hey, Mom, what's going on?"

"Hi mijo, I hope you're having a great weekend. Real quick, I'm calling to update you on the house situation. I've thought a lot about it and ... we've decided to sell. I know, I know, that's not what you wanted, but I think selling's the right move right now. Lance agreed. He said the market is—"

"I don't care what Lance thinks," I interrupted.

"Mijo."

"No, I've already told you I'm willing—more than willing to take it over. The house is all I have left ... all *we* have left of Dad."

Mom stayed quiet for a few seconds.

"I know, mijo," she said softly. "I know. But me and Lance—"

I hung up on her. It wasn't that Lance was white—he was—or that he'd become Mom's boyfriend six months after Dad's heart attack. It was his predilection to butt into our family affairs, offer his two-and-a-half cents when we were good on the money. Lance wasn't a bad guy, I don't think, but that didn't mean I didn't think him a snake slithering on my property. White people, like snakes, have no propriety when it comes to death and property.

I pictured myself stomping on a snake's head then sipped my black coffee. It was now lukewarm. It had lost its desired effect—to burn my tongue.

I went back to my book. I read a sentence six or sixty times over. I couldn't comprehend it for the life of me. Bolaño wasn't Balzac, but I might as well have been blind.

I put the book down again and closed my eyes. I focused in on the song playing in the back. "Maria Maria" by Carlos Santana. I started bobbing my head and was immediately brought back to middle school football, empty bleachers, being on bus rides with the boys. Falling asleep, drooling.

As Santana made his guitar sing, I placed myself in Spanish Harlem, like in the song. Maria Maria—*living the life like a movie star*. She was getting ready for our hot date, putting on her makeup. It was always me waiting for her, Maria. She took forever, always. "Beauty takes time," she'd always remind me.

How amazing would it be, I wondered, if even just for ten seconds I was Santana's guitar—no, his *fingers*, his magical fingers with so much talent they could make guitars sing and moan, just like women? What would it be like, I wondered, to have millions of fans across the world chant my name, beg encores every single steamy night like I was the god of music? Like I was ... Santana?

The song finished and I found myself tapping my left foot like mad. I was anxious. I needed fresh air. It was my day off, after all, so I needed to enjoy it.

The rude homeless man was sitting on the sidewalk by the Starbucks entrance. He looked up at me, studied me for two seconds, and seemed not to remember me one bit. He was whacked out.

Finally, he asked, "Got a cigarette I can bum?"

I was taken aback by the politeness in his voice. I patted the sides of my shorts where there were no pockets.

"Sorry, sir. Don't smoke."

"Geez, who you gotta blow around here to get a smoke? The Muffin Man?"

My muffin! I'd left it uneaten on the plate. Like my coffee, it was getting colder—was probably already cold. But then, the homeless guy. My sympathy synapses had already started firing. If I couldn't help the man get a smoke, the least I could do was feed him. Right?

"Hold on a sec," I said.

A few seconds later, I was back outside, objects in hand.

"Take this," I said, handing the muffin to the man, "and eat it."

"And take this," I said, handing him the coffee cup, "and drink it. This is my blood."

He accepted the muffin and coffee hesitantly. He sniffed the muffin, as if trying to detect poison. Then he threw it hard into the street. I didn't even blink. I watched the muffin get pulverized by oncoming traffic.

The man polished off the coffee in one swig, burped loud, then set the empty cup on the ground. He reached inside his camo pants and pulled out a crumpled cigarette and a lighter.

"You had one this whole time?" I said.

"Last one. I get 'em where I can."

My phone buzzed. A text from Vanessa.

I can't come over. Ted is in town the next couple weeks. : (

"Doomed!" the homeless man shouted. "We're all doomed!"

He tapped cigarette ashes into the cup. The Starbucks woman imprinted on it still smiled her green smile. I'd never smoked a day in my life, but in that moment, a cigarette sounded so good. Anything did. Anything but standing there with the crazy homeless man, thinking the thoughts I was thinking.

"Hey, do me a favor and toss this into the street, willya," I said, handing the man my iPhone.

He accepted it hesitantly then said:

"And what do I get out of it?"

I paused.

"Cigarettes and a cheeseburger," I answered finally.

He scratched his expired beef jerky chin.

"It's gotta be from Whataburger, though. I don't want no McDonald's."

I smiled.

"Deal," I said.

Without wasting any time he launched my iPhone hard into the street. It flew upward as though toward heaven then took a sudden cruel dive toward traffic. I saw it get obliterated. Smashed into a hundred little pieces. Nobody stopped. Nothing changed.

"Incredible," I said.

"That's my screwball. Pretty good, huh?"

"Fucking amazing," I agreed, holding back tears.

The Post-it Manifesto

∞

There are those among us who must destroy others as they do themselves. I was unlucky enough to experience this as a child, and to still believe this the human condition as a man.

I explored this idea last week with my wife over breakfast, offering my typically provocative writerly stance that the local bareknuckle boxing league that recently opened would serve as saving grace for some of our city's violently afflicted. Sandra disagreed, clearly bothered. I doubled down, threatening support of the league via donation. Sandra shot me a glare I'd rarely witnessed in our marriage, a look so primal I can only describe as it as lion-like.

"You know how I feel about violence, Nick, so I'd rather not get into that. I'm not one of your writer friends."

"Sandra," I said, "I was only pointing out the nobility of institutionalized fighting as therapy for victims. I didn't mean to offend you. And Jesus, you don't have to be so condescending. You know that's toxic for me."

The last part was dishonest; Sandra knew some of my best work was brewed from toxicity.

"It's always about you, isn't it?"

"Me?" I raised my voice. "Jesus, speaking of victims, look around you. Everything you see, I've done for you. Us."

She raised her hand to halt me, as though an SS officer cutting short explanation.

"Everything you've done? Like I haven't agreed to go half on everything."

No longer was I commensurate with reason.

"You want credit, Sandra? You want an award? Is that it? Well here's your award. Congratulations. I can't think of a more deserving person than—"

She splashed her half-full glass of orange juice on my face. My eyes burned. Disoriented, I heard stomping around upstairs. Then Sandra was back downstairs with her gym bag strapped on her shoulder.

"I'm off to my mom's," she said coldly, wholly unconcerned with what she'd done. "I'm probably staying the weekend, so do whatever you need." She slammed the front door before I could say a word.

How long I sat at the kitchen table, I'm unsure. After I finally got up to wash my caked face, I played a Sharon Jones record to calm my nerves. Entertainment seemed the only sensible thing to do.

Later, I swung by the used bookstore off Broadway. I browsed through the fiction shelves first, then poetry, then philosophy. Displayed eye-level on an endcap was *The Communist Manifesto*. Its positioning, coupled with the realization that my old copy had been lost—its contents long forgotten—persuaded me to grab it. Plus, it was only three bucks.

Behind the front counter, Mr. Torres must've whiffed enough foul air to play detective.

"Everything afloat, Nico?"

"Yeah. Doing fine."

"And the missus?"

"She's, uh, she left for the weekend." My tongue clicked harshly, irrespective of my control.

Mr. Torres smiled knowingly.

"The Manifesto, huh? Good choice. Have you read it?"

"Twice in undergrad, once in grad school," I answered. "But I don't remember a single word."

"I'm afraid that's the case with most books, my friend."

"Yes," I agreed.

"Tell you what. Since you're a fine patron, and an even finer writer, it's yours, no charge. I could use the money, but Karl Marx sure don't."

I left the bookstore with Mr. Torres' flattery putting me in the mood for Culver's, where I ordered a cheeseburger and a large chocolate concrete, which amounted to a stomachache. I wondered how I might have felt if an angel of death had let slip that that had been my last supper on Earth.

Once home, I took two Tums and brewed a pot of coffee to help with digestion. Meanwhile, pacing around the kitchen, I opened *The Communist Manifesto* and became enthralled by its opening line:

A spectre is haunting Europe—the spectre is communism.

Three pages later, I shut the book, disappointed by its form as a manifesto—by what it was not: a tale of specters.

Truth be told, the world of history and facts didn't interest me when life wasn't firing on all cylinders.

That night, I dreamt I was a specter—the Spectator of Bareknuckle Boxing. I was me and not-me, hovering over the missions and poorer neighborhoods of San Antonio like a vulture, senses attuned to action. Where dirty crowds gathered, I descended into. I placed bets on brutal fights. I swigged malt liquor and scarfed down nachos. I cursed bloodied losers. I flicked three middle fingers at the sky—one for my abusive father, one for my fallen wings, and the last one for Sandra.

The next morning, following a couple cups of coffee, still dwelling on the bizarre dream, I grabbed a stack of yellow Post-it notes on the dining table and jotted down words, then sentences. After some time, I filled eight Post-it notes with tiny handwriting. Surprisingly, what developed was a declaration, a manifesto, to Sandra. Despite my belief in the evolutionary function of violence, and despite my upbringing—Sandra's, too—I wrote that I would always protect our future children from that poor, nasty, brutish world right outside our loving home.

Then, as if on cue, a text arrived from Sandra. She'd return in the evening. I prepared our dinner: spaghetti with sliced chicken.

As soon as she walked in, I pulled her to me and, with Sharon Jones & the Dap Kings serenading us from the record player, danced with her to a few songs. Dinner passed comfortably.

In bed, I awaited Sandra's reaction to the mini manifesto I'd positioned on her jewelry case. She clipped coupons robotically, not once indicating intent to speak. Since it wasn't uncommon for me to initiate conversation, I did.

"So, did you see my notes?"

"Mhmm," she answered, clipping away.

"You read them all?"

"I did."

"And?"

Without stopping her activity, she replied, "It was very nice."

It was very devastating, really.

"That's all you've got?" I inquired, trying to sound unhurt.

My desperation warranted a concentrated glance from her.

"Oh Nick," she said, stroking my chin. "Always the writer with your questions."

She kissed me on the cheek and soon shut off the lights.

"Goodnight," she said.

"Goodnight."

Sandra was instantly asleep, I wide awake. It was only nine o'clock on Sunday. It was all too much.

I went downstairs with my Post-it Manifesto and started typing it out from my MacBook.

After additional editing and further plot development, a magazine would publish it, and in a few months, I'd have a bonafide meta-novel in my hands. It was, after all, my responsibility to sharpen my craft, to write everything down and to pay most of our bills.

Gun, With Zero
Music

∞

1.

What else do you need to know besides that I hoard napkins and Fire sauce packets from Taco Bell? That I love frequenting the little Thai joint on the corner of Mulberry because the cute Indian waitress thinks I'm hilarious? That I was unable to finish psychology at community college because I'm super ADD (like for real)? That I'm almost 36 and still living with Mom even though she's been dead for 10 years? I can still hear her bragging to her chubby church friends about my marginally inspired newspaper op-eds. She'd called them "those adorable little stories." No aptitude for distinction, that woman. Oh, proud Mother. RIP.

I was never cut out for the military like Pops. He'd finally realized that when I turned 15. I swear his disapproval of me propelled him into the tattoo parlor for the second time where on his other forearm they needled in a busty mermaid. He'd put in 25 in the Navy. I can't believe Mom didn't kill him before she went and murdered herself first. Oh, Father, who art on Earth, unhallowed be thy name, thy grossly inked sagging skin. Please stop texting me. Amen.

Who I have been conversing with lately, willingly, via text message, is a woman, I think (she must be!), named Fiona, who for fun plays bass in a punk rock band called Benito because apparently she's the great-granddaughter of Mussolini—illegitimately, of course. You know the old joke, dictators thinking mostly with their ....

Fiona and I are scheduled to meet next week. Jesus, I sound like a shrink! Correction: Fiona and I arranged plans to meet next week. Our dialogues—yes, I can categorize them as such because I'm archiving them in Word documents—to my surprise, have gone quite smoothly. Very little exertion on my part. This is how Fiona entered my life: I'd sent out the same generic text to 5 random numbers—call it phishing, judgmental reader—and 2 months later, now, shabam: Fiona. Oh, Fiona, your trusting nature and spunky wordplay have churned my tortured soul, my heart full of holes, my heart full of microscopic worms carving it away. You've branded me, Fiona, like a ranch cow. I think I almost might love you to the *mooooo*n and back.

2.

I must confess, prior to my last entry, I'd thought journaling was only for people of weak disposition. Whiners, complainers, crybabies and the like. But nobody other than my therapist had ever mentioned it'd be so *joyous*. To label keeping a diary cathartic, an exercise in therapy, just doesn't do it for me. It softens me down there. I'm not some little boy who feels the need to retaliate against the page all the injustices this world has inflicted upon him. And there have been many, make no mistake. But alas, I'm a big man. I take life's punches on the chin, smile, then ask for seconds. Pain is tasty to me, like a Snickers bar. Thick, nutty, appropriately gooey—lots of calories for such a small package, but ultimately sweet, character-expanding. Size XL T-shirts are my jam.

Dad texted me today insisting we meet for lunch ASAP. He said he wanted to catch up to discuss "important family matters." What that translates into is a major league lecture he's itching to unleash on me. I'm in no mood for that. Never will be. "Go get another tattoo," I wanted to message him back. "Another double D broad somewhere on your chest. Or maybe on your lower back. Just let me die in peace with your surname. Isn't that sufficient enough?"

Instead, I actually messaged him, pathetically, "K. Get back 2 u soon." It's sometimes best to keep official business vague.

3.

Mom doesn't approve of Fiona. She still speaks to me in dreams. Lately, it's happening at a higher clip.

"Don't waste your time on her," she warned me last night. "She's up to no good, nothing but trouble, that devilish tramp."

I must confess, I've never been 1 for listening to Mom. I've been a fairly decisive lad since hopping out her womb. I think on my own, and on my own 2 feet. I answer not to God, country, nor parentals (dead or alive), but rather to myself in the mirror. When I ask me, "Are you talkin' to me?" I say to me, "You bet your ass, me."

Fiona admitted she's excited but nervous for our upcoming meetup. 2 days! She said it's crazy when you really think about it. 2 complete strangers agreeing to see each other in this day and age. I texted her, "So then think of me as a 1-night stand. It's more socially acceptable that way." As anticipated, she responded accordingly: a smitten-face emoji, followed by an eggplant emoji. She's a freak that way, Fiona. But she's my freak. She's Fiona.

4.

Meeting Dad for lunch was a huge mistake.

No, opening up to him about my love life was. Every time I give that old dog a whiff, I'm swiftly reminded why I ought not to.

"Are you out of your country-fried mind, son?" Dad lectured. "How old are you again?"

"I'll bring a gun. Relax. I have to stop by Academy anyways."

"You know, listening to you sometimes is like watching a train wreck in slow motion. Let me help you, son. Please."

"Farewell, Rear Admiral," I said. "God bless thee."

He texted me an hour later. "At least use my handgun. Ol' reliable. Save your finger-licking $$$!!!"

Oh, Father, I suppose this progeny of yours is still obliged to honor you.

5.

I wasn't sure if it was a sting operation or a setup to jack my wallet and car. Either way, pictures of my penis were involved. I realized only at the scene—of course only at the scene—that I'd never confirmed her age. Never had her send me pics. Never asked to FaceTime her. Nothing. Love, it blindfolds and triple-knots.

I parked my car and waited anxiously by a bench near the playground entrance. A few minutes later, she materialized out of the darkness, out of the trees. Scared the fuck outta me! Her greeting was high-pitched, girlish. Not the Fiona I'd imagined. Not Fiona, I determined. Oh, snap.

As I backpedaled to my car, regretting having worn a black turtleneck, a large figure—a man, I'm certain—burst through a bush and sprinted toward me. Later, I checked Twitter to make sure it wasn't Chris Hansen I'd plugged. (Relax. That was a joke. Sorta.)

My father's target-practice training instantly kicked in. Remember, it activated itself—I didn't act volitionally, I declare.

3 rounds were fired quickly. Bam bam bam. The figure

dropped, the girl shrieked. Instinctively I collected the spent shells, then ran to my car and got the hell outta Dodge.

The first thing I thought was, You would've made a damn-fine Seaman, boyo. Hooyah!

My recollection is it was extra shadowy that night. A classic noir flick. I remember the clouds, not seeing the moon once. The saturation from the streetlights overwhelmed me. But I had to keep driving. I was both me and un-me. I was high—stoned on the villainous rush of escapade and 21st-century dating gone wrong. Very, very uber wrong.

I cried. Sobbed like a gentle-hearted cuckold. The music was off. Had never even played.

I was heartbroken. An inconsolable killer.

6.

It's been 2 days and I haven't heard anything from anybody. Not 1 peep.

I've contacted the local county court about the process for changing my name. I should have all the necessary documentation.

I feel paranoid, panicked, greasy. Duped and betrayed. Mom scolded me big time last night. Dad wants to meet again. He said he wants his gun back. He'll know it's been used. He's super NRA like that.

Oh, I've really screwed the pooch royally this time, haven't I? Haven't I, dear reader?

That was a rhetorical question to me. Me, please don't answer me.

Me, please don't judge me.

∞

Pepperoni

∞

When people ask me if I believe in God, I sometimes say yes. I sometimes also say no, because that's what I've come to realize. But it's safer to say yes. You get less stares, don't have to explain as much, as if you called somebody's mom a ho.

I used to stack boxes with a dude named Alvin. I was nineteen when we met. He was about twenty, twenty-one, black, tall, skinny, white pimples hella across his neck. Fool was quiet unless you got him started on the Dallas Cowboys or Jackie—his supposed ex who had his baby.

Working with Alvin all day, I got to know him. He'd stash his pocketknife and joints in this little slot he'd cut in the side of his black Air Force Ones. I can still picture him looking up at me after I'd catch him, goofy ass tryna act like he was tying his damn shoelaces, playing down that ingenuity. One night after our shift, we took our shirts off to see who had a bigger chest—no homo. This was back when I did a thousand pushups a day. Homie's nipples were huge, like the pepperonis you get at Subway, except black.

"Damn, son!" I said.

He punched my arm hella hard then put his shirt back on. That's when I started calling him Pepperoni. He laughed, but said it was the most fucked-up moniker of all time. He said that malarkey had better stay in-house. He used corny words like that.

Pepperoni rode the bus to and from the warehouse. He couldn't afford a car.

"Not even a Cavalier?" I asked him once. "Look online, homie. Kelley Blue Book."

"Cabrón," he said—he'd call me that because I'm Mexican in appearance and attitude—"I couldn't even afford gas for a fucking Vespa if Santa brought me one for Christmas. Chingao."

One night I offered to give Pepperoni a ride home, but he said naw. The next night I insisted, but still naw. The next night I was like, Homie, I gotchu. Hop in.

"All right, cabrón, all right, don't get your chones in a twist," he said.

He said to drop him off at the corner store on Rittiman, that he'd walk home from there.

"Walk home? What am I, the VIA bus? Just let me drive you home, fool," I said. Because maybe he'd invite me to smoke up.

He said his neighborhood wasn't "precisely safe." Said it was "rather treacherous." Air quotes.

"The Valero's fine here, cabrón," he said.

"Really, dawg?"

He stayed quiet, just stared out the window like he was searching for somebody. Message received. I was only human, so I left him with:

"Prideful pepperoni-looking-ass motherfucker."

"Gracias for the lift," he said, tipping an invisible hat.

The next two days he didn't show up to work. Didn't call in. Didn't text me or anybody.

Turned out he was shot the night I dropped him off. The night I fucking left him at the store. An investigator—that's what she called herself—stopped by the warehouse to break the news, ask some questions. She said it was probably a wrong-place-wrong-time kinda thing.

"C'est la vie," I remember her saying. She didn't seem bothered one way or the other.

God, I thought. I couldn't believe it.

Seems like half my life has passed me by and I still can't fathom this shit.

C'est la vie.

Sometimes I say to people, "Sure, I believe in God, yeah."

I bet ten years from now nobody'll remember Pepperoni except me. I bet hardly anyone remembers him now. His custom Air Force Ones, his huge pepperoni nipples I can't unsee. I don't know where they buried him, who his family is. Nada. Sometimes I dream about visiting his grave, catching him up on all the malarkey that's gone down. Pouring one out on his headstone—cliché, I'm aware—watching the sauce soak into the dirt. I don't think that'll ever happen. I know it won't. Believe that.

Do I believe in messiahs or saviors? It took me a long time to comprehend that I'm still here, and if there's one thing fucked about this duplicitous story, it's that.

That I'm still here. C'est la vie.

Angels and Elves

∞

The angels and elves had stirred up trouble again.

It was snowing in San Antonio, coming down hard. It blanketed highways and backroads, downtown and even the two acres of dirt south of Broadway that would soon become another shopping center. I wondered how many more poor people that would push further south. I wondered how many of them would be alive by next Christmas.

A 500-year event, the weatherman said. But people here will tell you—just ask them—they remember January 1985 like yesterday; kids sledding in driveways, young men firing snowballs at their crushes, snowmen bumming rides on the backs of pickup trucks, dogs licking up melt across from the Alamo.

I looked outside the fingerprinted window at Whataburger and thought, You're somewhere else. Then the same old strain on my neck.

The migraine was coming.

I sipped coffee and flipped another page of my book, Sam Shepard's final novel, *Spy of the First Person*. He'd died back in July. ALS. Didn't tell nobody. Death is like that sometimes.

The book, my first by the steely-eyed actor-author who would act and write no longer, was on top of my notes. I could barely stand them anymore.

I read because my daughter loved to read, and she read because her daddy did so. Who was modeling who?

"Last Christmas" blasted from somebody's phone. My mind drifted back to the start.

This too shall pass, I thought. This too shall last.

Flash.

They killed him, the blind man who ran the ramshackle shelter on Zarzamora. Shot both his useless eyes out, stole his wallet, Rolex, a couple cheap paintings and a few bags of donations. Used clothes. They left him like a piece of trash. I told myself a long time ago I should've went into journalism. As if that would've been any brighter.

The blind man was a widower, a pastor. He ran his shelter with his daughter for ten years. Good man, she called him. They handed out little green New Testament Bibles to addicts, pampers to single mothers. They were usually one in the same. Kids.

My guess is it was a jealous boyfriend, a baby-daddy who was Blood or MS-13. But that hardly made sense because the blind man, Mr. Reyes, dead on arrival, was in his seventies, no record. His daughter was divorced, college educated, also no record. She was tore up when she said who could do something like this. And why? I was embarrassed to admit I asked myself the same things—asked myself the same things every day.

I checked my watch. Five till ten. Time to head home. Good thing since the words on the page had become just words on a page. Once the migraine hit, I'd be out of commission.

I gathered my notes and downed the rest of my coffee, which gave me a shot of nausea and goodwill. I was two or three steps outside Whataburger when I looked back and saw an old man and an old woman slowly approaching the door. They were tiny, barely five feet tall, barely could walk. She was the one holding him up.

"Allow me," I said, holding open the door.

They looked up at me with trepidation, then worn-out smiles.

"Thank you very much," said the woman.

"You're very kind," said the man. "Good people here in San Antone."

I nodded and thought, If only you knew I missed my daughter's birth, that I dream about having been there to cut her cord.

When I think about her infancy, I see her fingernails, small and lovely, insanely delicate in design. It blows my mind not enough parents relay this to their children.

Walking back to my truck, the snow crunched under my boots like cockroaches. I felt my hair getting wet. A 500-year event, they said. Enjoy it while it lasts.

I started my truck, put my palms against the air vents blowing heat.

Where I was parked, the highway—410—appeared as a giant gray serpent jutting out from the ground. From hell. My mind had long thought weird like this. The shrink said that was okay. People are the weirdest creatures of all.

Staring at the tall highway, which looked like an ungodly roller coaster, I remembered where I was headed. I let my hands warm up some more and then put my truck in Drive. I checked my phone. A few missed calls from the station, a text from Karina from her mother's phone.

Daddy it's snowing!!! I miss you.

She was with her mom this week, probably next week, too.

Miss you too, princess.

I drove through the flurry and thought, You're somewhere else. Then I asked myself at some point, "Will you be pushed further south too?"

"Way down south," I answered. "Way way down." The shrink

said it was also okay to answer your own questions. People are very, very weird.

Before the migraine knocked me out—it was starting to squeeze the back of my eyes—I was sure I was in Chicago, or Detroit, or New York. Yeah, I was in New York, where the snow and the dead piled as high as the Empire State Building. "Let them live," I heard the green woman called Lady Liberty say. "Let them die—I don't give a shit." My mind was talking crazy again. Good thing I was almost home.

What I want you to know about the night it snowed in San Antone, December 2017, is how the snowflakes shined like pale diamonds in the streetlights. God, so gorgeous. The kids would remember it for the rest of their lives. Tell their kids and their grandkids. They'd pray from the pews for another night like it. Maybe our Lord and Savior would listen. A 500-year event, they said.

The next day, by noon, all the snow was gone. The dead blind man greeted me at my desk bright and early. His files were there with the others, getting cold. Colder.

I remember thinking with a lingering migraine pinching my eyes, Before I'm done here—before I'm pushed way down south—I'll get to the bottom of this. I'll find the answers, the angels and elves will throw me a bone. I'll make Mr. Reyes' sad daughter proud. I'll make my own daughter proud. I'll stick around for the next big snowstorm, Karina in my arms, enjoying the snow globe all around us, two children singing.

Blind

∞

I shot the blind old man in his face cuz I was scared they'd do me the same. I screamed at him it's you or me, I'm sorry God, old man, but this is my life, no one showed me the way, Mom and Pops have been dead these twenty-one years so I sucked black poison outta the world, became a proud and violent son making thugs in stolen J's my fathers, and how I landed here on Zarzamora Street, this shithole with strangers with holes in their veins, is beyond me.

I don't ask questions anymore, don't pray. I eat the time I got left so it's go go go. One thing led to the next and my boss Mario tells me, threatened me really, you better take what's yours—ours—don't you for a second tolerate an ounce from him, that old fucker who turned my mother away, that devil with God's tongue passing out His books like a pious king. You're gonna punish him right and good tonight, Mario said, his daughter too if she's around, they've had it coming all their lives.

That's when I knew, that's when I knew, Mario was possessed and blood or no blood this was my life, the boys, Zarzamora. The Alamo. The Dome and every murdering piece of scum fighting for breath and scratch cuz it's them or you, us or you, and the choice is made already. I squeezed the trigger and boom boom, it was done, he was done, his blind eyes no longer of the earth.

I jacked all the shit I could from his shelter and busted out running and as I hauled ass I noted the weight in my arms and thought, said to myself, this is the price of life, mine too, hatred serves two masters but one in the same, the wicked and the selfish, nothing else matters, it was me or him, me or him always, God destined it this way, I played my part the best I could.

Then it snowed. It snowed crazy like a motherfucker and damn was it beautiful. For my troubles Mario gave me $200, said, you done good tonight, kid, you made it rain, literally, go and celebrate, build a snowman, rest up, we got work tomorrow. I stopped by Whataburger and ordered a double, ate it right across from some tired-looking dude who smelled like a cop.

After I finished but before I could do anything stupid I got up outta there and wandered out in the snow. For once that night I cracked a smile, cried a little bit—yes, I cried. I remember thinking, the sky cries too, it hurts tonight, it bleeds. It's burying every one of us in powder, millions and millions of crystals like falling little stars. God. How the stars fell in my eyes.

In Space, Your Meals Are Determined by Hired Cooks

∞

I pressed my palm against the reinforced window in my bedroom. The glass felt cool, exactly like they felt in my previous life. The difference was that on the other side of this glass, there was an infinite and ever-expanding black canvas. It was filled with mostly nothing, and we knew mostly nothing about it. This put me in a mood.

I removed my hand and focused on my ghost-like reflection. My face glowed amber, a result of the Himalayan salt lamp on my nightstand. My eyes, naturally dark brown, were reflected on the window as small craters—appropriate given my state. I tried to grasp reality—that what I saw in front me took eighty milliseconds to process into consciousness, that all of boyhood was believing in invincibility.

Two small hands wrapped around my waist, gripped me comfortably.

"What're you doing, baby?" my wife's voice asked.

"Zoning out," I answered, caressing the tops of her smooth hands.

"Beautiful out there, isn't it?"

"That's one way to see it."

"Well, don't mean to interrupt your meditation, Mr. Space Philosopher. Dinner's ready in five. We're having Mexican tonight."

"Didn't we have Mexican last night?"

"No, Guatemalan. There is a difference."

I didn't feel like spinning this into a big deal—I easily could have—so I said: "Thanks for letting me know, sweetie. I'll be out in a bit."

My wife kissed the back of my neck and I heard the satisfied patter of her footsteps.

Mexican, Guatemalan, it didn't matter. Our dinners were at the mercy of a professional cooking staff. All the cooks appeared Mexican, though one was white for sure.

I selected a random point outside my window to home in on—probably an unmapped coordinate of space irrelevant to everyone except to me.

I fixated on the point with laser focus—a sea creature spotting his prey from a distance.

An announcement briefly stole my attention.

Attention passengers, this is Chef Johnny speaking! Tonight's main course will feature enchiladas verdes, brown rice, black beans and flour tortillas so soft my dear abuelita would've had a cow! ¡Perfecto! For dessert, tres leches cake prepared by yours truly! ¡Delicioso! Don't miss out! Bring your appetites and your maracas!

As I continued fixating on a piece of unidentified space which I knew to be much older than anything on Earth, I felt something inside me unspool, like a piece of fabric undone by someone pulling a loose string.

We were having Mexican tonight. We'd had it last night. I was sure we'd have it tomorrow night, and the night after. These decisions were outside my control, as were so many others. What little choice I'd had, I'd given most of it away. For what, exactly?

Then, for a split second—scarcely longer than a blink of an eye—I hated my wife. Hated her unequivocally. Gazing into space, into the cold oblivion none of us knew a thing about, something crossed my mind, what needed to be done. Drastic. My hands trembled.

I closed my eyes and touched the window again. The glass, of course, was cool, its cool familiarity assuaging my nerves.

I was resigned to Chef Johnny's enchiladas verdes. And to whatever else was whipped up. In space, it is always night.

Mexican, Guatemalan, it doesn't really matter. It's always night in space. In space, your meals are determined by hired cooks. There are worse things.

An Exercise in
Futility

∞

"I appreciate that," said Simpatico Allan Lima—Sal—to Tim Warner, who was holding open the elevator door.

"My pleasure, sir," Tim Warner said.

Class act, thought Sal. I guess what they say about this kid is true.

Sal got to his desk and waved his hand over his computer. He was greeted sardonically, per usual, by Lightspeed, his American Indian operating system.

"How," Lightspeed said. "Ready to take a gander at these emails, Sunshine?"

"Hit me, Chief," Sal said. "Hit me hard."

But first, a joke, which Sal was hardly in the mood for. Lightspeed didn't take the hint.

"So this Indian guy returns some toilet paper to a salesclerk. The clerk says, 'Apologies, amigo, no refunds on poopoo tissue. Them's da rules.' The Indian says, 'I've been vulgarly misled, sir, and demand my money back. There's a rash on my bum.' Clerk says, 'Misled? A rash? Explain yourself, buster.' Indian says, 'The brand here says Angel Soft, but it oughta be called John Wayne.' Clerk says, 'John Wayne? What're you getting at, pal?' Indian says, 'Cuz it's rough and tough and don't take shit from no Indian!'"

Sal was promptly e-blasted by seventy-eight unread messages, the first of which was from Venus Luna, his boss's secretary. Not the worst way to start his day.

Hi, Sal! The cryptocurrencies were transferred at midnight. The Gramboldians will be very happy. Thank you for all your hard work! You're amazing.

Sal smiled and thought, It's true, I am. He cracked his fingers and typed a response in the air, wearing a satisfied smile.

V, glad we can put a fork in this project. The Gramboldians have been a pain in my hiney for so long I've gotten used to the ache. Speaking of fork, how about the two of us finally try out that Greek place we've been talking about? The one a few stations from here. Tomorrow, noon?

Two minutes later, Sal received confirmation from Venus. Yeah, definitely not a bad way to start the day.

Feeling exceptional—perhaps it was also the organic orange juice kicking in—Sal powered through his emails till lunch.

Later, Sal's boss, Michael Gordonnn—yes, three n's, don't ask why—president and CEO of the company for all intents and purposes—swung by Sal's desk. Gordonnn noticed Sal's head swiveling every which way, his hands and fingers swinging every which way like a mad pianist, which could only mean one thing: Sal was taking care of business.

"Powering through?" Gordonnn interrupted.

"Correctamundo," Sal answered.

"Dammit, Sal, you're an inspiration, a maestro, the only one around these parts, other than Venus, with a real armpit for elbow grease. Hear that? You made my spirit animal croon." Gordonnn had a knack for strange expressions. They amused Sal in the early years, but now he was indifferent.

"I appreciate it, Boss," Sal said.

"As far as I'm concerned, anyone who staves off the Gramboldians is Employee of Eternity in my book of platonic love letters. You make me proud to wear my sleeve on my heart." Gordonnn took a contemplative sip of coffee, savoring that poetic low-hanging fruit.

"You flatter me, Boss," Sal said plainly. "I'm blushing."

Ten hours later, Sal was cooked. Lightspeed reminded him that he still had a body to nourish, and that it must be nice to go home to such a lovely warrior queen.

"You're glitching," Sal snapped. "That was my past life. I roll solo these days. Catch ya later, Chief."

Sal left his office and put on his space suit. He hopped inside his mid-size Cruzer de la Crème and zipped over to Franky's. He'd worked up an appetite.

"There's the Homo sapiens of the hour!" Franky greeted Sal as he entered.

"Frankito," Sal replied. "What's cooking, you big handsome blob?"

"Number one, tons of pickles, no mayo?"

"That's why you keep me coming back," Sal said, shooting Franky a friendly finger. "You take extra special care of me."

Sal dropped a fiver in the tip jar and could tell that the big purple blob known as Franky was all smiles. Let it be known, Franky hardly ever smiled.

"I appreciate your business, my boy," Franky said.

"No no," Sal countered. "Correction: I appreciate *your* business."

Sal cruised home to the music of Gang Starr, his favorite hip-hop duo of all time. Hearing Guru's crafty New York-centric rhymes over jazz-infused beats, spun by none other than DJ Premier, reminded Sal of Earth, his planet, the place where he'd never been to but where people like him came from. Sal experienced the pangs of nostalgia. In this moment, hip-hop felt oddly, coldly, out of place in space.

At home, Sal devoured his delicious sandwich in silence. He

enjoyed hearing the sounds of feasting. Of crunches and munches, gulps. The melody of eating was the business of being alive, and in the blackness of space, you often lost sight of that.

Sal's phone buzzed. Annoyed, he waved his hand over the device. He was acknowledged, per usual, by the ever-faithful Lightspeed.

"How, Sunshine," Lightspeed said. "Urgent message, Playa Hater. You might wanna check this out."

"Who from?" Sal grumbled.

"Who else?" Lightspeed answered.

But first, a joke, to which Sal refused, to which Lightspeed insisted, to which Sal acquiesced.

"Knock knock."

"Who's there?"

"Indian."

"Indian who?"

"Indian we're all minorities in space. Get it? *In the end* we're all—eh, screw it. Your message, Your Majesty."

Sally, I don't know what the hell happened, but the damned Gramboldians rejected our payment. Talk to me! What in rapture's trashcan is going on?

Sal sighed; he'd had a bad feeling about this, but ignored it. He knew never to ignore his instincts.

Sal cracked his fingers and typed a response—it looked like he was tickling the air.

"Go easy, Sunshine," Lightspeed said. "Don't lose your cool, Sheriff," he added. "Scalp all their repugnant asses and send me the pics," he whispered with glee.

I'll handle this. By tomorrow, the issue will have been resolved.

Sal swallowed the last of his now-cold sandwich, washed it down with organic orange juice. The juice tasted a skosh acidicy.

Sal walked to his closet, knelt, then removed a square piece from the wooden floor. He closed his eyes, recited an old prayer his grandmother used to say before bed.

In Sal's hand was a small piece of jet-black metal, unmistakably an ERX-007—nicknamed the Anti-Newton in the black market because it was the only weapon in the known universe capable of destroying matter.

How and why Sal possessed the gun is a story for another day.

Before leaving his apartment, Sal went to his kitchen and opened a drawer. He wasn't about to forget his trusty pizza cutter.

Sal had no qualms preparing Gramboldian pizza. In fact, he'd tried it before, and it was the closest thing in taste and texture to pepperoni pizza.

Sal's palate was an equal-opportunity employer.

Yeah, Sal thought, if they don't play nice, then at least I'll know what's for supper the rest of the week.

A thought entered Sal's mental periphery, one that inherently prefigures decisive action. Sal summoned Lightspeed.

"How may I be of service, O Herculean Exterminator?"

"Instead of 'Indian we're all minorities in space,' how about, 'Indian we're all John Wayne in space?'" Sal suggested.

"Nope, doesn't work, doesn't make any—oh. Never mind. I get it."

Sal smirked and so did Lightspeed. Let it be known, it was technologically implausible for Lightspeed to smirk.

· · ·

A whole month went by without Sal stopping by Franky's, so, it was no surprise to see the owner ecstatic when his favorite patron walked in. The Prodigal Son himself.

"There's the human of the hour!" Franky greeted. "It's about time you showed your stinking meat suit around here!"

"Frankito," Sal greeted. "Sorry I've been away. Work's been killer."

"Don't apologize, my boy," Franky the purple blob said. "I'm happy to see you alive and well. My, you've gained some weight, man! What's that about? Please tell me you haven't found a finer eatery than mine, you scoundrel?"

Sal patted his paunch and laughed. His clothes had certainly fit tighter. A good decleansing was in order.

"Too much home-baked pizza," Sal admitted. "I swear to the Milky Way if I see one more slice, even smell it, I'll puke my guts out straight across the galaxy."

Kolson

∞

Back when I was at the Academy, on the outskirts of the Red Asteroid Belt, I bunked for six months with a trainee whom I can still say, with absolute certainty, is the most remarkable person I've met. His name was Kolson, or, at least that's how I've remembered him.

Every night before lights out—though we always had, out there, the suspicion that lights were out no matter when—Kolson, that bizarre entity, would bend my ear trying to convince me that he truly wasn't Kolson, a man born on Praxis-7 the night of Moonseve, but the fragments of other souls long since passed. A living, breathing amalgamation of others, but not Kolson, who was only "an idea"—his words.

Kolson had Germanic features—dirty blond hair, a strong sharp chin. He once said he remembered living a day as Stan Lee, the creator of Spider-Man, in New York City in August 1962. The smell of sweat and sewage, gasoline and popcorn. Kolson claimed he not only remembered living as Stan Lee, but understood what it meant to live as Stan Lee.

145

"Since the golden age of comics, us boys, all of us of the human race, have never ceased modeling our behavior after the superhero," Kolson said. "Even now, when heroes are no longer necessary."

"Shut your mouth and go to sleep," I said.

It got better; by better, I mean batshit crazy.

One night, Kolson said to me, to my complete befuddlement, that he knew what it was, how it felt, to play chess against Einstein—yes, Einstein—as Garry Kasperov. Or Bobby Fischer. Or was it with the left brain of Bobby Fischer and the right brain of Kasperov?

"His wit—their wit—my wit!—is short distance, like a sprinter with massive quads," Kolson said matter-of-factly. "Think Usain Bolt. Whereas Einstein's wit, akin to a bicyclist, is small and spindly. Long distance. Remember reading about that guy Lance Armstrong? Remember him, that cheating bastard from Texas."

"They must've poisoned your make, you're talking like a drugged lunatic," I replied after a loud yawn. It was only much later that I recalled I'd never seen Kolson eat.

"I don't own any part of Christ's soul, though, don't get me wrong," Kolson said, changing the subject nonchalantly. "That would imply I possess God, and if you understood what it was to live as Albert Camus, or Friedrich Nietzsche, or Stephen King, Stephen Hawking, Genghis Khan, Jorge Luis Borges, that blind genius, or even Yuri Gagarin, who was betrayed by God, you'd know then that God's little more than a kill switch in our readily corruptible brains. A pawn invented for the game of domination."

Deploying a different tactic—and what was about to be mentioned has since stained my mentality like a cancerous sore—I asked Kolson:

"And myself? Do you know what it means to live as me?" To which I added: "Do you own a piece of my soul, Kolson? Do you, you slimy snake?"

In utter darkness, in lights out, somehow still I saw—I swear—a grin so enormous it beamed, emitted its own perverted light.

"Salinas, my brother," he said regally after a short silence, "remember, I collect the dead souls. When the time comes, long after yours cuts its tie, you can ask me that question again."

After the Academy, we each went our separate ways. Three hundred young graduates shipped off in three hundred opposing directions, glorious assignments in hand. *For the betterment and advancement of humanity*, they had droned into our heads.

Needless to say, I've never again seen Kolson (although the French literary theorist Roland Barthes wrote that "never again" is an expression reserved for immortals). Still, the likelihood of a reunion is virtually nonexistent. A shot into infinity, eyes closed.

But every once in a while, when a streak of red light slices across the cosmos, I still have trouble sleeping. Because I'd be lying then if I claimed a part of me doesn't feel, beyond reasonable explanation—awful, terrifying conviction—that I could be, I might be—totally, categorically wrong. That the universe in its cold majesty has revealed its true face: a bottomless bag of stars, white-hot knives. Multiplying blades.

Thrown in the bag, swimming for an opening, meager breaths, restricted air, it's only a matter of time.

Kodak Moment

∞

Donny stared vacantly at his estranged uncle Lorenzo.

He noticed how makeup had tried to mask his uncle's dark-skinned goateed face. It looked made of candlewax.

Donny was in this same position last week, peering down at his uncle, but not in a funeral home. It was in the backyard of his childhood home on Bluegrass, where Lorenzo had once downed brisket and beer at barbecues.

In the dream, Donny's uncle had sat upright, clear fluids trickling from his wide nose. He Medusa-stared directly at young Donny, horrified.

"C'mere and shake your uncle's hand, hijto," Lorenzo had said. "Be a good boy, respect your ol' uncle in all his shining glory."

Donny walked away from the body toward the exit door. Before he left, he turned around to face him one last time. The man who was gone so long, discussed behind closed doors so much as though he'd rammed their minds with a sharpened stake.

Donny's heart pounded furiously. He felt as if the beats in his throat came from an absurd bongo. But it wasn't music.

He jammed the nails of his pointer fingers into the fleshy bottoms of his thumbs, half expecting something to happen.

Later, after Donny had swallowed three Ambiens and was under the covers, he was certain he'd seen his fingers wriggle. Eyelids flicker. Adam's apple bob.

He understood from experience that these convictions would soon pass, two days' time. They were tropical storms, these foolish delusions—unruly, spiraling, then out of this world. It was the stuff between cyclones—the supremely real center—that kept him guessing if the plane that carried his weight existed on its own accord, or on the agenda of something so ancient that to dwell on it was to beg for its slow crawl, arrival, destruction of naïve order.

A terrible burden for anyone to carry before bed.

Close your eyes, Donny. Sleep tight. Let the waves wash over you, this time of healing. The dead remain silent. Tomorrow the earth will be merciless. You'll remember its rage. It's the living who wail when they're awake.

Chicken Run

∞

"Bunny, don't be on your phone while you're driving."

"I'm not, Mom. Just looking for a good song."

"Same difference."

"I'm thirty years old."

She glanced at her, then reached out and covered the top of her cold hand gently. Her bones felt as slender as cheap chopsticks. She remembered back when, as a little girl, she used to hold her mother's hand during mass. It felt different then. Larger, warmer, alive. Everything did.

"How about some 50 Cent?"

"You know I love me some Fiddy."

When she pulled into the narrow drive-thru at Church's Chicken, the glowing yellow sign reminded her of a micro sun, the way it beamed arrogantly against the night sky. These were old stomping grounds. Yet, everything felt unreal.

"Can I help ya?" said a man's bored voice from the intercom.

"Yeah, let me get a ten-piece special with a side of mashed potatoes and mac 'n cheese."

Though her eyes registered the dark figure lurking by the passenger side of her SUV, her heart didn't explode until a few seconds later. Her mom shrieked as though air had been sucked from her lungs.

The thin man wore a Spider-Man T-shirt with holes all over. His hair was long and matted. His beard too. He looked darker, Mexican, but you couldn't really tell at this time. His eyes were deep set. Familiar.

She remembered the scorching summers when she'd see him march up and down the main farm road every day, barefoot. Nuts. That was years ago.

"God, he's still around?"

"Yeah," her mom answered. "He's gotten worse since you left."

He glared at her with black, insane eyes, then growled like a rabid dog. She remembered being chased once by a dog. He was as huge as a grizzly bear. Thank goodness she was on bicycle.

"You ain't kidding," she said.

"He's kookier, but he's harmless, the poor guy. The police leave him alone. We all do."

The chicken couldn't come fast enough. As they waited, he did too, glaring. Snarling.

When she drove off, she kept her eyes on the rearview mirror. She watched him disappear—fade away, really.

The roads were empty. Past eight o'clock, this town slept hard.

The ringing in her head put her in a mood.

Stupid as it sounded, she imagined herself turning around and offering the man a few pieces of chicken. Asking his name. Giving him some cash. If handed a few bucks, she believed he'd do the right thing—save them for a hot meal.

Dumb as it sounded, she pictured herself also shaving off his filthy beard. Back in college, several times she'd shaved the faces of her boyfriends, out of curiosity, mostly. They liked it. She got so good at it she considered becoming a barber. The only woman in a men's shop, swiping clean the male flesh roughened by stubble. Seemed to her a real woman's job anyway cleaning up men properly. Also, to be the one holding a blade against their necks.

"Bunny, please slow it down. You're going a little fast."

Not fast enough to escape her tiny cubicle, the anti-anxiety pills, the drink. Debt. Overlit offices, day in day out. It might have been some indefinable force—God, they all say—that had relegated her to this scene.

"Bunny."

She had decisions to make—most pressingly the one facing her now. Who knew what would be the right thing? That could only be judged later.

Music playing, foot inching down on the accelerator, both hands smothering the steering wheel, she heard a whooshing sound fill the closing-in space between her and the passenger seat. A noise not open to being quieted.

She looked to the right and held her breath. On the passenger seat chicken bones were piled in a small mound, like a cairn on an old trail. She wasn't full but her fingers were greasy. The last time she checked, she was only a voice. She had to reconfirm from time to time because she still forgot.

Her foot dug down; the engine roared. Nothing else there in the blackness. Nothing at all.

Except the music, and the voice, and it whined:

"Bunny!"

The Wrestler

∞

I like to wrestle. You can't say horseplay anymore after the Penn State thing, creepy Jerry Sandusky—people look at you funny. But wrestling, it's just fine.

I have big, long legs and big arms—thanks, Mom and Pops—so I'm practically engineered for wrestling. I have about a hundred brothers and sisters, and I'm one of the youngest, so guess who everybody's punching bag was? I used to watch wrestling for hours and hours—WCW, WWF, Hulk Hogan and all them. I used to get stomach rashes from lying on the carpet all day. I had this giant Andre the Giant stuffed toy I practiced my piledrives on. I turned him into a pile of cotton before long. My pops would get home late and wrestle with me. I accidentally broke his jaw once, but it was all in good fun. Nobody got hurt. In ninth and tenth grade, I made the wrestling team and I got pretty good, but had to stop before eleventh grade because I ended up cracking a vertebra. Not gonna lie, I was torn up about that for a good long while. I made peace with it, though. Had to. Professional wrestling, it just wasn't in my cards.

I still like to wrestle and probably always will. That doesn't mean I'm a violent guy. Only once have I thought about shooting a dog and that's because he was plain mean and bit my finger clean to the bone. Then there was the time we whooped up on my friend George's pops. His pops was always wasted, knocking him around like a ragdoll. He'd banned George from swimming at the public pool because he said George had "zero business swallowing kiddie piss." George's mom was Vietnamese and his pops was white and ex-military. One night while he was asleep and snoring like a drunk Neanderthal, George and me snuck into his room wearing hockey masks and kicked him around good. I felt awful about it, his squealing rerunning in my head for a day or two, but I never heard any more noise about George's pops after that. Problem solved. Although George and I stopped trading Game Boy games and we went Amber Alert on each other's lives.

Honestly, though, I wouldn't hurt a fly. I'm being serious. I'll squash me some mosquitos due to mad cow disease and malaria and them being the deadliest creatures on Earth, but otherwise, why else would I entertain senseless violence? For the heck of it? Just for show?

There was something my pops used to say that I'm a big believer in:

"Can't spell 'harmony' without 'harm'!"

He meant that in a funny, motivational kinda way. And he was right. But nobody should get the wrong idea. You have to be super careful with people nowadays.

I guess that's maybe my whole point here. A guy like me who indulges in a little horseplay—a little bit of harmless wrestling—is slowly getting cornered into the turnbuckle day by day. Where's my representation? Where's my seat at the table with tree-huggers? Abuse is wrong, no doubt about it, but corporal punishment surely isn't lest God strike me down this second. Rotten kids never not benefitted from a good spanking! My pops would whoop me on the butt three times—the last spank for good measure—if I misbehaved, and look how I turned out. Respectful of authority, perpetually in good standing with the law. You can try to politicize me, but for your information, I voted for Obama twice. I ain't no Tea Party tool like that doofus Ted Cruz. I fulfilled my civic duty gracefully, like Shawn Michael's Sweet Chin Music, so don't come barging into my house with garbage about my politics otherwise.

I love my wife, Daniela. Dani. She stole my heart the night we saw Rage Against the Machine. You should've seen her throw down. Who knew that tiny woman packed heat like "Macho Man" Randy Savage! Of course, we were younger then. Stupider. We don't do stupid stuff anymore. We can't, not with our son Eli, and our jobs. We're getting too old and savvy for stupidity.

So, if you can, imagine how really, really, *really* excited I was the other night when wrestling came on the TV and Eli was watching it with me and he asked me to teach him a move. I looked at him and thought, That's my boy! Then proceeded to put him in a half nelson.

"This is a half nelson," I said to him, "but for your opponent, it's full pain!"

I guess I might've gotten a little too rough because when Dani came in, she screamed at me to let him go.

"We're fine," I said, pinning Eli's head to the ground, "this boy can take it."

I don't remember how it happened next because it was so quick, but Dani tried to break us up and somehow, in the heat of the moment, I guess I got too riled up and pushed her off accidentally. I guess there's no stopping a man's adrenaline. That's biology for you. She flew back like Eddie Guerrero and hit her head on the coffee table. Before I knew it, blood was everywhere. We're talking a Ric Flair level of blood.

I finally let go of Eli and told him to run and get bandages from the bathroom, then I crawled over to Dani and stripped off my shirt and covered her head with it. She had a nasty gash on her.

I felt awful, like my whole body was a sack of bricks.

"I'm so sorry, baby, I'm so sorry, I love you, I love you," I said.

Next thing you know we're at the hospital. Not gonna lie, I told them the "Stone Cold" Steve Austin truth. I was embarrassed, as embarrassed as I've ever been. I said we were horsing around, that it was only an accident. Dani wasn't talking, so thank God she didn't contradict me.

As me and Eli sat in the waiting room, waiting, he tugged my shirt.

"Pops, is Mom gonna die?"

"No," I answered, "Mom'll be just fine. It was all an accident. We were just horsing around. Your mom's a tough woman. Exactly like Ultimate Warrior, but the lady version."

Then Eli said something that damn-near chokeslammed my heart. Still kinda does.

"Can't spell 'harmony' without 'harm'!"

Followed by:

"That was a good half nelson, Pops!"

I looked at him and smiled. I thought, That's my boy, and patted his head.

And that's the kicker about this crazy world we call home. You've gotta be prepared for anything. Literally anything. Bob Dylan said it best. The times, they are a-changing. The trick is—and there ain't no faking around this—you've gotta have all your countermoves pre-planned.

Chipped

∞

And there I was, about a month ago, having another phone conversation about my infidelity—as opposed to what, fidelity?—the inexplicable choices I made, those selfsame choices I must—we all must, at some point—answer to, holding a coffee mug, or some other terrible excuse for a birthday gift for my mother, when I spotted, at a distance, Chip Engelland—yes, Chip Engelland, the world-renowned shooting clinician for the five-time world champion San Antonio Spurs.

Chip Engelland—the guy who singlehandedly redoctored Tony Parker's jumpshot! Who every day stared up into the stoic eyes of Tim Duncan, my sports hero growing up.

Chip Engelland grabbed a book off a display, thumbed through it, then looked up in my direction, at me, quickly; a sightless glance, the kind one delivers to strangers thoughtlessly. In the next second—or was it shorter, that instance?—Chip Engelland put the book down and walked away, his lengthy legs swiftly transporting his body like a bullet train, like it was nothing, effortless, like I was some good-for-nothing nobody—like nothing was nobody's business—nothing *is* nobody's business, right?

The space between Chip and me spread rapidly. The distance between us, myself and the decorated assistant basketball coach, grew long, wide, wider, then chilly, like the aftermath of a macabre river massacre.

I'm not sure—how could I be sure?—if you've ever read a novella by Patrick Süskind called *The Pigeon*, about a Parisian security guard who one day encounters a pigeon in front of his apartment door, the sight of which, in that moment—that instance—hurls him into a nightmarish existential crisis. The Germans: they write this kind of drivel, the type in which Gott isn't pulling the strings.

Now call it what you want, dear reader—no, I'll call it what I want since it's *my* story—but Chip Engelland walking away from me that day in that moment—that instance—in Barnes & Noble about a month ago, slicing off our connection, injecting impossible stuffing into the geography separating our bodies, was in my mind my ... pigeon moment. Yes, I'll say it: Chip Engelland is a flipping pigeon! His wiry legs, his flowing white pigeon wings swept him off to destinations unknown, and I, like a low-grade security guard, a rent-a-cop who knows not one iota about self-defense nor the finer points of safeguarding the inner workings of my eggshell brain, bumbled epically.

How delicate a creature is the German. How delicate a creature am I—a thirtysomething San Antonian learned in English history, less so in the language of my culture. Even less in the important field of knowledge of Keeping My Marriage Alive.

I must've uttered strange utterings because my wife—we're separated, by the way—asked me over the phone:

"Sorry to interrupt, but what does your grandmother have to do with us?"

"It's the carpet here inside the store," I said, thinking on my feet. "It's green, *Great Gatsby* green light green, the same color the carpet was at my grandma's when I was a youngin."

"I miss her too, your grandma," she said civilly. "I do. But that's not what we're talking about right now."

"I was going to say," I said, changing the subject, "I just saw Chip Engelland. You know, the shooting coach for the Spurs?"

"What?"

Case in point: I'm cursed with the uncanny ability to string together doomed combinations of words at the worst times. If only the sweet essence, the saccharine juice of thought inside my nucleus, could be rightly dispensed.

"The thing is, honey," I said, unable to contain myself from deploying the pet name, "I'm not a bad guy, and I don't want you to think I am. I feel like complete dookie today. I love you, honey—I love you so, so much, with every ounce I'm made of. But what can I say? I'm a man and I effed up. I'm a freakin' moron. And now I'm dragging my feet around this bookstore like a nincompoop, a ghost, a dumbass rumor. Wait, I don't mean it like that," I said. "I'm not trying to make you pity me. Please don't pity me."

"I don't," she said acidly.

The brief hush afterward sunk in, somehow, bitter-sweetly—super-duper heavy.

"I'm a colossal failure, always will be," I said, surprised to find myself holding open a book of love poems by Pablo Neruda. "Guess what I have in my hands."

"What now?"

"The book I bought you the day after our wedding. The one I read to you deep into the night."

Silence, then, "Fuck, dude."

A jazz song saturated the bookstore in a sterile, concealed mist. A Weather Channel kind of number.

Then my wife said something priceless before releasing an awful blitzkrieg of brutality—a machinegun fire of poison-tipped sentences she'd never be able to take back, nor would she, the punishment of which I'd deserve for all eternity.

"How's the song go, 'Love's kinda crazy with a spooky little boy like you,'" she said.

"Yes. Groovy song," I said. "Good ol' Dusty Springfield."

And before I had a chance to recite to her, for the last

time—for old time's sake—a young Neruda love poem, before I had the chance to explain to her what it felt like to cross paths, ever so briefly—for just an instance—with a coach from my favorite NBA team, she ripped me a new one. She ripped me a new one good, for the ages.

Boy, did the wound gape.

My heart spilled over messily like a water tower punctured by a bazooka missile.

Then I fell—no, I dropped, no, I stumbled, no, I tumbled, nosedived, cannonballed—yes, I fell in love again—again—for the thousandth time.

The Consideration

∞

My name is Larry Rios. About myself, the only things worth mentioning are that I'm divorced, my parents have long been in the grave, I'm an autodidactic philosopher, and I spend practically every minute of free time with my nose in a book.

Last year, I discovered a small used bookstore on the Eastside, not too far from Big Lou's Pizza—an overrated pizza joint if there ever was one. The bookstore, at that time, had been in business for only three years, which I'd learned after striking a conversation with the owner.

After I mentioned to the old man my passion for tackling challenging literature, the classics, philosophy, he asked me if I'd ever read Jorge Luis Borges.

"Of course I've heard of him," I replied brusquely, quickly realizing I'd answered a question he hadn't exactly asked.

He smiled knowingly, his wild bug eyes twinkling in the light, then he said, "Wait a minute, please."

A moment later he returned with a paperback in his mummy-like hands—what turned out to be a beat-up Penguin Books edition of Borges' *The Book of Sand and Shakespeare's Memory*. The cover art, in black and yellow, reminded me of a gentle bumblebee, or rather, a hellbent hornet. Ironically, it consisted of a honeycomb-esque arrangement of butterflies.

Handing me the slim volume, the owner said, "On the house, I know it'll satisfy you."

His inscrutable kindness still strikes me as a quality rarely found among our kind.

Allow me now to cut to the chase: I read the book in two days, that very same weekend, so that it wouldn't occupy my headspace upon my return to work on Monday.

In four sittings I devoured the book, which is really two books in one. So dazzled was I by the prose that in those two days, I ate only two meals daily as opposed to my usual three.

Of all the tales in the book—that dangerous object disguised as merely one thing—"The Disk" stuck out considerably, like a large purple coin among pennies.

Three pages long, "The Disk" is narrated by a hermit woodcutter who's visited one day by a dethroned king. The king briefly reveals to the narrator, from the palm of his hand, an invisible one-sided disk; instantly obsessed by the mystical object, the narrator asks the king if he could have the disk, to which the king rejects him and swiftly leaves his property. In hasty revenge, the narrator buries his ax into the king's head, forcing the disk's ejection from his hand. The last line of the story reads: "I have been looking for it for years."

Weeks passed and try as I did, I couldn't extract from my mind the impossible image of the one-sided disk. How any person could flush out such bafflement, such nonsense, such derailment from his mind was beyond me. Perhaps only a blind man such as Borges was capable.

Among the last promises I made to my ex-wife, Lucia, was to quit smoking. To my credit, I hadn't taken a drag in two long years. However, not a month passed after I finished the book when I drove to the corner store and purchased a pack of Camels. The familiar burn.

In bed I thought, Perhaps days are one-sided, perhaps air is one-sided, perhaps the moon is one-sided, perhaps the soul is one-sided, but not a disk. Never a disk!

During work one day, I googled the words "comprehension" and "philosophy" and stumbled upon a thread discussing how objects are defined—with an "intentional definition or an extensional definition." In other words, according to one contributor, "the comprehension of an object is the totality of intensions."

What, then, is the totality of a one-sided disk if its other side is rendered nonexistent? I say "rendered" because I'm now aware of the sly invention of such an object.

Late one night, with a cigarette dangling from my lips, I stepped into my bathroom and spoke into the mirror. It occurred to me instantaneously, horrifyingly, that asking a question to my reflection yielded only one response—the selfsame question—which would forever remain unanswered. Then soon forgotten.

This happened next, and is unbelievably true. I lifted the pair of grooming scissors and with the resolve of a seasoned surgeon gently traced, with one of the blades, the outline of my face, slowly. The sensation of the cool metal tickled, gave me goosebumps.

"Perhaps my face is one-sided," I said to my double, as a madman might say.

I called Lucia in the morning and thanked her profusely for all the years she'd put up with me—with my silence, with my isolation, my violence, my melancholy.

"It's only now, for the hundredth time, that I see clearly the gemstone you are," I told her. "The memory of you keeps me breathing."

Brief silence, then she said plainly, "You're smoking again, Larry. I can taste it."

It took that conversation to jolt me into action, and the first thing I did was return the Borges book to its rightful home. I had, and never would, any claim to anything given to me for free.

When I arrived at the bookstore, I searched around for the old man, but was intercepted instead by an old woman.

"May I help you?" she asked me kindly.

"I'm here to return this to the owner," I said, tapping on the book's front cover. "Do you know if he's in today?"

My words had an awful effect on her, for her face, upon hearing them, sagged deeper toward the lifeless tile.

"He died last month," the old woman answered solemnly. "He was my husband."

Somberly, I offered the widow my condolences. I didn't have the heart to give her the book, so I placed it on a shelf discreetly then exited the store as unobtrusively as I could.

Day passed into night, quietly.

Later in bed, I couldn't help but think to myself, as if beyond my control, as if landing on punchlines to tasteless, horrible jokes: Perhaps life is one-sided. Perhaps death is one-sided. Perhaps God is one-sided ....

The Yellow Slide

∞

Between segments of so-called reality captured by my eyes like film, pearls of the past still manage to, on occasion, slide through my silver screen, interrupt my viewing experience with dictatorial selfishness. In this way, these pearls are no different from mama ducks marching their ducklings across a busy country road. They don't ask for permission.

What I'm getting at is, I thought about the yellow slide today.

I hadn't thought of it in forever. To my knowledge, the yellow slide hadn't bore a sizable dent into my identity. Hadn't contained poisonous metaphysical ingredients with which to dye my soul blue. That's azul in Spanish—exquisite word, isn't it? But there it was, stubbornly jammed between two of my brain folds, its seat at the cerebral table reason enough, so to speak, for its assertion of dominance. Disruption.

I should've let it go at that, but no, we know that isn't how the mind operates—that faulty label gun, slapping on meaning—so-called significance—to things real and unreal, sometimes to noxious effect.

170

This morning, I had to check a voicemail left overnight by a demanding yet wealthy client. After I keyed in my passcode, my phone's internal operator—a shrewd housemaid of a voice—informed me that my phone was filled to capacity, therefore I needed to delete some of my saved voicemails. I swear I heard her add at the end of her demand, "Or else."

In the process of deleting voicemails—a vacuous activity apropos my generation—I relearned two insignificant facts: 1) Melissa Guzman was responsible for 80% of them, and 2) Melissa Guzman was hysterically consistent in her salutations, practically a robot, like my shrewd housemaid internal phone operator

Voicemail Number One: "Hi Andre! This is Melissa Guzman calling from Schumann and Schwartz."

Voicemail Number Two: "Hi Andre! This is Melissa G. calling from Schumann and Schwarz."

Voicemail Number Three: "Hey Andre! This is Melissa calling from Schumann and Schwarz."

Voicemail Number Seven: "Hi Andre! It's Melissa, Melissa Guzman, calling from Schumann and Schwarz."

Somewhere between Voicemails Number Eight and Eighteen—somewhere between the Melissas—I abruptly found myself at the entrance of the yellow tube slide. That is to say, at the doorstep of a reconstruction of a memory. I was on my back, reading Sharpie-scribbled writings on the ceiling of the yellow slide's wall. I was eight years old again.

The wall's inscriptions presented to me a new world, a startling world I'd never before imagined from my bedroom. And though that world was new, I was frightened to learn it was also ugly.

Written on the yellow wall were black letters, which formed words strung to other words—altogether a crude ink-pearl necklace of harsh phrases that penetrated my sponge conscience. Reading them aloud, alone, I knew the sounds coming from my mouth were wicked, would get me in big trouble if I repeated them in other places I roamed in the world, my old world.

The writings covered a lot of ground: human private parts, which were also generously illustrated, naturally. The n-word. *God hates Mexicans*, written so stylishly it had to be by the hands of a girl, maybe a friend of mine. Then there were the words that softened my bowels: *I will find you and kill you.*

I sprinted like Speedy Gonzalez—God's and my country's detested Mexican rat—from the playground to my grandma's house across the street. I didn't stop to look both ways.

My grandma wasn't particularly affectionate, but she must've sensed something was wrong. Perhaps she felt guilty for letting me go to the playground unchaperoned. She popped a frozen pepperoni pizza into the oven then told me to sit with her as she watched her telenovela. She brushed my hair with her thick fingers. I noticed above her TV the old portrait of her and grandpa, both impossibly young and familiarly unsmiling. The whole time we waited for the pizza to finish, my arms were locked around her tiny waist. Though I wanted to, I didn't cry. The new evil world, dead as it wished me to be, wasn't enough to make me cry. That's the important thing to remember here. So says I.

• • •

This afternoon, on the way home, I entertained a seemingly unprecedented thought—at least to me—a radical thought that, written out now, seems utterly ridiculous: Does God actually despise Mexicans? If Trump was God, man being made in His image, the answer was transparent.

I laughed out loud and, after I turned on my radio, to the tune of Pitbull—Pitbull!—I nearly swerved my car into oncoming traffic. Of course Pitbull had unknowingly answered my unspoken question—Pitbull, who wasn't even Mexican, who I could clearly picture in my head swaying to the thumping beats of reggaeton, his black-gloved hands pumping the air as if he were milking the very teats of heaven.

But somehow, my ridiculous question still required my answer, because once I posed a question—even if unspoken—I was the one needing to answer it. I recalled three women, all Hispanic, whom I'd been with in relationships—one disastrous from the start, two pretty good until the end. Then I forcefully remembered that I, a college-educated, gainfully employed, marginally in-shape, lifelong tee-totaler of a Hispanic, a Mexican American, *still feared God*, therefore and henceforth must be loved by Him. I may have sprung from an illustrious line of unhappily married people, but they were all faithful, as was I. Life was to be good. I was headed home, after all, in a brand-new Range Rover.

The gratification of my answer lasted only a few minutes, the yellow slide having wedged its way into my psychic web. It was now a member of my random-access memory, very possibly at the forefront of my thoughts. How long it'd be there, how long it'd haunt me, how was I to know? Temporality is as slippery as it is foreseeable.

Thinking better of it, the yellow slide was—and is—my childhood at my grandma's. There were times, when she wasn't soundlessly mourning her husband, when I wasn't at the playground and instead at her house, that she'd remove her dentures and chase me into one of the bedrooms, hollering all the while like a witch. That's bruja in Spanish—ghastly word, isn't it? I'd lock myself in whatever room and stay put there for the rest of the day, listening in for her hyena cackle. She scared me. That woman, my grandmother, she scared me.

Let me revise myself from earlier.

Most things, probably, like the yellow slide, stretch themselves over time—mushroom into caves, tunnels, empty chambers of what you later realize is a giant revolver. And before long, now that I've dragged a gun into this story—specifically, my grandma's old regular-sized detective special—a sensible decision must be made:

Inch inward into the darkness and drink from it, or acquaint my soft temple with a cold, hard bullet.

Rice Krispies Treat Conundrum

∞

Sitting on my ivory throne, reading Christopher Gilbert poems, eating a Rice Krispies Treat, I blow crumbs off my countertop.

A single sugary rice grain remains—halfway on the countertop's edge, halfway from falling into the at-capacity trash bin. At gravity's mercy.

The odds! I marvel. I couldn't repeat this if I tried.

Suddenly I'm back in class, in the back row, the backs of studious heads sizing me up. Pop quizzes. *Gravitational constant times mass divided by distance equals force of gravity.* Blah blah blah. You know I Ask Jeeves'd that shit.

Then there were my cheap Sanyo headphones, Linkin Park's *Hybrid Theory* growling into my brain, an inflamed case of the bacne, Mr. Jenkins' pale hairy gut bulging out of his size-small Abercrombie and Fitch polos, Columbia and her perfect white teeth, her brown M&M eyes. Her budding breasts. Jesus. Distractions, sirens, the lot of them! Will this portal ever close? Will bygone days ever leave me be?

The hanging sugary rice grain speaks up, and before I can freak out I remind myself I'm tripping. Its voice is soft, like Crispin Glover's. It says to me, in nearly a whisper, "Hey, c'mere, come closer, please."

I, uneasy, lean in. "Yes?" I inquire.

"Being pushed to the edge, and not a nanometer farther, is a numbers game," it says. I can barely make out its mouth, this teeny-tiny little slit. "You've been playing it your whole life and didn't realize it. I've the math to prove it. Check it out on my pocket calculator, which to you probably looks like an atom."

"Stop it," I beg. "Don't ruin my life for me, you big stupid little liar! You trifling chimera!"

"You are unoriginally repeatable," it judges, "a set of equations, simple arithmetic, and don't you forget it, you overexcited self-absorbed pothead."

I sit up straight and feel a slight headrush, my lower back achy. I try to comprehend I've just been schooled and burned by a punk-philosopher food item. A wee parcel. But I'm tripping.

And I get it. As with anything else, this game we're in is all about asking the right questions first. Because equations without formulas—discoveries without intent—are merely unremarkable accidents. Incidents, minus context. The trick is knowing there's no room for magic in this world of the slowly dying. The briskly vanishing.

I make another brilliant breakthrough, pat my own back at my moment of clarity, then cough. And cough again. That's all it takes to cut off my train of thought.

What the hell am I going on about? I think. I'll never arrive again at this teetering-grain result, at least not in my life-time. The event came, then went, like everything else that's happened to me. By tomorrow, I'll have eaten more frozen meals, fake-listened to more people, solved more of my own petty problems before the next wave attacks.

Space Invaders. Life, baby. Rinse and repeat. Rinse and repeat! How's this for an equation: The living divided by the dead times three hundred sixty-four (the purported number of licks it takes to get to the center of a Tootsie Pop) equals the nature of reality, quantified.

Constant change—accept it then lean into it, like I did with my edible little friend.

A banging on the door.

"You still in there? God help me, how long can a man poop!"

"I'm reading!" I shout at my wife. "I'm getting to the good part! This is Me Time!"

"Whatever, I can smell the weed all the way from the kitchen. How much longer you gonna be?"

"JUST A FEW MORE PAGES!"

I hear her sigh, patter away. Wives' retreating footsteps: the glorious but momentary soundtrack of respite for husbands abroad. Nirvana forbid this husband's spouse (read: one hundred thirty-seven-pound ball-and-chain) ever catches on.

I'm being unkind. Even in my altered state, I'm cognizant of my fortune having a caring mate such as mine providing asylum from ghosts of My Past. After I'm finished here, I'll puppet her around the living room, as I've developed a habit of playing from my phone Roaring Twenties jazz songs on YouTube and from behind my dearly beloved piloting her noodly limbs wildly to the music. It's amusing for both parties. Try it out on yours sometime, health and inner weather permitting.

We all must figure out—on our own—how to best navigate toward the inevitable.

Welp, I think, Me Time's over. Was splendid while it lasted.

I wrap what's left of my roach in toilet paper—a conservative two squares because it's Charmin Ultra Soft—and slip it under the rug. I suck in all the oxygen I can manage and blow that Last Grain Standing to kingdom come, which is somewhere behind our combination washer and dryer. I mock-whisper to it, to great satisfaction, "Who's repeatable now, bitch?" Then I flush the toilet and wash my hands.

Discretion

∞

How's this for discretion:

During my lunch break, I was gassing up at the ghetto Walmart off Jones Maltsburger when a scarecrow-looking white dude approached me and asked me for money. Shameless, both his large filthy mitts cupped, he never let up on his hobo frown. All that was missing from his getup was clown makeup. Regrettable, I thought. If only dopes like you could afford Juilliard.

The homeless man's dog-sad eyes nonetheless burrowed through my hardened mask, injected my inner gears with a horrible chemical grandmothers call empathy.

But rude hearts such as mine? They aren't easily won, if ever they can be. In other words, a nasty idea popped into my head, and I was determined to breathe life into the sucker *because I could*. Because what Edgar Allen Poe had written was true; the sinister spirit of perversity floated around us always, lurking, searching for delicious vessels. And once it chomped down, it clamped to the bone.

Anyway, you know what they say about tan-skinned people—they taste exactly like chicken.

"Under one condition," I told the homeless white man.

"What's that?"

"I film you for a quick video for a Twitter account for my part-time job. A short message. I tell you what to say and then you repeat it. Got it?"

"Whatever, man, as long as I get paid."

Somewhere in the soft Midwestern gut of America, an ethics professor's waxy ears prickled. Hell, here in the city, the air was ripe with Catholic culpability. For hundreds of years, ruling priests had done what they do: guzzle the wine-blood of our innocent youth, nibble the host-bodies of willing adult sacrifices. (Spoken like a true-blue angsty Catholic schoolboy.)

Me, I was thoroughly going to enjoy reclaiming my time guilt-free.

"This currency," I said to the homeless man, handing him a $10 bill, "having passed through hands slick, greedy and black-market, is a contract, our agreement, your word made sacred. Do we have an understanding?"

"Okie dokey," he said, snatching the greenback like a seagull seizing his lunch.

On his second try—yes, he was that good, polished, professional an actor as any I'd witnessed—he stared straight into my microscopic lens and delivered his lines perfectly, powerfully, with no nonsense and the brand of ruggedness evoked by a Hollywood leading man from a bygone era—think Jack Palance or James Coburn—except more emaciated and much more butt-ugly.

"To my esteemed president of this United States of America," the man recited, "my country, my home, I present to you myself, me, Carson Williams Jr., homeless white man, overlooked garbage, the real pus of this pilfered landfill. Judge me all you want, Holy Emperor, Supreme Commander, Majestic Wig. But open your cataract eyes and see: none of us, especially not pieces of trailer trash like me, live free. I once crawled out of my mother's ivory womb privileged—and ended up pillaged. God bless you, sir, and God bless America."

That was all I expected out of my willing participant, but in hindsight—ah, that's where our true wickedness lies, in hindsight—I'd've pumped three more videos out of my dirty little natural.

Driving back to work, to my main job, fighting the insane lunch-hour traffic of fatsos on the loose, I called my ex-wife, put her on speakerphone.

"Hello?"

"Hey, what's good?" I said.

"Hey. Um—I'm at work right now. What's up?"

"Oh nothing. Just called to ask you a quick question."

She stayed quiet so I cut to it.

"Why'd you recommend me for the communications gig at the church?"

"What?"

"The part-time job at our old church. Why? You know I'm not very religious. Very evangelical."

"Is this really why you're calling? I have a feeling it's something else."

"May you please answer my question? I've gotta get going soon."

"You know I don't like when you put me on the spot. I figured the extra income would help you pay for ... you know ... the therapy."

"Wonderful," I said. "Thank you so much for your honesty. You've always had such a big heart. By the way, did you know that *therapist* with a space after the *e* spells *the rapist*? I must be the millionth loon to have figured this out today. Have a fabulous nightfall!"

Five seconds later, predictably, she called back. But I'd already received the push I'd craved. It had stewed and bubbled inside me, the hate, and all I'd needed for it to leap out was a small wind. Got it.

I recall pondering just then the shakily discernible difference between the words *dissociate* and *disassociate*, drawing

blanks, then settling on the word *diss track*, a purely distrac-
tionary stopgap plugging the futile rift between the etymo-
logical diastema. (The last part is thesis-paper-speak for a
gap between the teeth—do you fancy punching mine out?)

On Saturday morning, inside the empty administrative office
annexed to the church, not only did I post the video from
their Twitter account, tag The Donald, I messaged it to other
parishes. One by one, I searched, I uploaded and I sent. How
easy it was, how satisfying it felt to heat up some monstrous
server in a ginormous storage room in Silicon Valley—all
the while outside the sun shined, cardinals chirped, Starbucks baristas brewed, hipster engineers sipped, and homeless people—the white ones, especially the whities—shat
their already-soiled sewed-in-China-or-Mexico-or-India-or-
wherever-the-people-are-dark-and-destitute pants.

Believe it or not, love it or hate it, I'd performed a public
service, issued a much-necessitated PSA. Through exploita-
tion, I'd exposed something beyond naming, yet undoubtedly
responsible for the woeful wasteland we'd dubbed wonder-
land, where even in its grease pits the Wi-Fi was free.

The blaze from the fallout was spectacular! You couldn't
fathom, or maybe you could, just how many randos liked
my tweet, loved my tweet, retweeted my tweet. Tweet tweet
tweet!

The day after I was fired from both jobs, I made the news,
was granted a ridiculous platform to speak my case, defend
my outrageous actions. I couldn't help but think: How come
someone so stupid, so smart, so brave hasn't already done

this? How come some other dodo from the inside hasn't already blown a hole in this ancient creaking galleon? Does no one loathe their ex as much as I do mine to produce a stunning cannonball splash in the wide-open ocean of faux civility? In this crumbling city, I suppose not. Disappointing.

A moment of silence, then, please, for you poor souls who allow your poor souls to be pooped on with or without your permission. Amen.

Now for a happy ending. The day after I was canned, effectively turning my ass into a local infamous celebrity, but probably effective only for a couple weeks, I was at home with a mad sweet tooth. I tore open a bag of Double Stuf Oreos and devoured all of them, washed 'em down with half a gallon of milk. It was as if I'd forgotten my age. I couldn't recall the last time I'd eaten so many cookies, a whole package by myself—probably not since the night of the big reveal about Santa Claus.

For two or three awful seconds, I regretted *everything*, a huge knot twisting, turning, churning my intestines.

Then I burped. Burped the loudest, slothiest, dragoniest burp one can imagine. I'm certain my upstairs neighbor felt the rumble and shut down his World of Warcraft campaign and called his girlfriend to be comforted by her cutesy anime voice.

As punishment and reward for my blockbuster belch, I retasted a thick creaminess—gross, I know, I know, but nonetheless delightful, the satiating full-blast milk-and-

Oreo flurry from the just-passed past. I chuckled, patted my fattened belly, and I thought:

Yeah. Ruling priests. Freaks. Captive souls, the lot of you. Do what I want. How's that for discretion?

Family Feud

∞

When the bus dropped me off, I checked the mail as I always did for Grandma. In the stack, there was a letter for me, which felt odd and exciting. Letters don't come often for most sixteen-year-olds.

It was from Harvard.

I brought the envelope close to my face and inspected the logo. The crimson shield was unmistakable. So were the words *Harvard College Office of Admissions* next to it.

I tore open the envelope and read the first paragraph. I was accepted.

After I learned that I'd aced the SAT, the first thing I did was go online and apply to Harvard. It took forever. The fee was $60—I had to use my grandma's credit card, but I paid her back with money I'd saved mowing lawns in the summer—but of course, I had the feeling that I'd just wasted my time and money after I submitted the application.

187

I burst through the screen door to find my grandma on the couch watching *Family Feud*. She was picking at one of her big-toe nails with her finger. Her eyes were laser-focused on the television.

"Grandma, I got into Harvard! I got a letter from them!"

She kept her eyes on the TV.

"Harvard?" she asked.

"Yeah! Harvard!"

"What do you mean you got in?"

"Well, let's see," I said sarcastically, "I applied online. They reviewed my application. They accepted me. Then, they informed me of their decision via mail."

My grandma finally looked at me.

"Don't talk to me like that, young man."

"Sorry."

There was a brief silence. I heard John O'Hurley's rich, baritone voice from the TV.

"Why Harvard?" she asked.

"What?"

"Why Harvard? I mean, it's wonderful they accepted you. It

really is. And you've always been a helluva kid, but still. Harvard is just so far away. And expensive."

"Grandma, it's not like I'm leaving tomorrow."

"I know that, but still. I thought you wanted to stay local?"

I'd never said that.

"Well, now that I can go to Harvard, that's where I wanna go."

"I understand, but is that the right choice?"

She must've noticed the frustration on my face.

"Look, sweetie, I'm not saying you're too young to be thinking about college. Not at all. But do you know how much Harvard'll cost? We don't have the money to send you to places like Harvard."

"That's what scholarships're for. I've gotten some already, remember?"

"So right now, would they even cover your meal plan at Harvard?"

Now I was really upset.

"Bad joke, sweetie, bad joke. I didn't mean that. Look," she said, shutting off the TV with the remote, "staying local just makes more sense to me. Harvard isn't for people like us. Hell, why go over there and pay them an arm and a leg when you can probably get a free education here? *Free*."

"Are you serious?"

"Listen to me, sweetie. I'm telling you this because I care for you, I love you. No one'll love you more than me. I want you to consider staying close to home. What if you go to Harvard and it doesn't work out? You'll be alone. I'll be alone. And we'll be slapped with a huge bill."

"And if it works out?"

My grandma smiled, as if she'd rehearsed her counterarguments.

"The thing about big ideas, sweetie, is they're like weeds: Once they start growing, they keep growing until you're all tangled up in them. Your grandpa had ideas, 'course you were too young to remember. He wanted to be mayor of this little town. One day, he was convinced God put him here to wear the hat. He told me that just about every morning. He wanted to do something great. He was so obsessed with fulfilling 'God's plan,' he spent most our life savings on the campaign. When he lost, it killed him. All for nothing. That's big ideas for you."

She paused. I stayed quiet.

"When I say I'm looking out for you," my grandma continued, "I mean it. It's just you and me now, sweetie. Do you understand that?"

I realized the letter was still in my hand. She never even asked to see it.

"Loud and clear, Grandma," was all I said.

I walked away to my room. I anticipated she'd apologize and call me back with food.

"Sweetie, I'm sorry. You know your grandma likes to talk too much sometimes. Look, let's celebrate with your favorite: a chocolate Pop-Tart!"

I shut my bedroom door, dropped my backpack to the ground, and threw the letter on my bed. I got under the covers and stared at the ceiling. There was nothing there I hadn't seen a million times, so sleep came fast.

I was at the top of a snow-covered mountain. The sky was beautiful and blue. I must've been thousands of feet in the air. Below me were clouds. The scene was breathtaking. I took a deep breath of crisp, cool air and exhaled white smoke.

Suddenly, a tangle of black weeds slithered up my body and into my mouth. Where they came from, I had no clue. They gyrated like a sinister octopus' tentacles. I started to gag.

I tumbled down the mountain with the fury of an avalanche. My view, obscured by the crosshatch of weeds, changed from white to blue countless times.

I woke up with my shirt clinging to my skin.

For a second, I thought the ground was snow, but realized, with relief, it was just the old cream-colored carpet.

I sat up and scanned the bed for my letter. I couldn't find it.

I wondered how long I was out. It was still daylight. I heard a shrill laugh come through the walls. It was my grandma's laugh. Was she still watching *Family Feud*, picking away at her hideous toenail?

I decided to take her up on the chocolate Pop-Tart. They really were my favorite.

I'd look for the letter when I got back.

Milkshake

∞

I'm the kind of small-town Texas guy who's believed in God his whole life. Where I came from, the order of things was God, then family, then football. That's just the way it was.

Everyone I grew up with fell into that order except a kid I remember named Tristan Goldsmith. "You won't catch me dead in a church," he once sneered to a group of us in the school playground.

Instead of tossing the football with us, Tristan would collect rocks in little tin cans like he was an amateur geologist. He and his family eventually moved away. Nobody could've cared less. That's just how it went.

I learned about Jesus Christ from my mother reading New Testament passages to me at bedtime. That's how a lot of us heard about the poor fisherman from Nazareth.

"I want you to become a good, hardworking man like Jesus," my mother would often tell me.

It was right after I graduated from high school when my mother got breast cancer. I was getting off work one night from the Coca-Cola plant when she called me. She said I needed to come see her soon, that she had bad news. So I went over to see her that night.

She was lying on the left side of her bed, alone, as she had done for seventeen years. She was wearing her same old faded blue nightgown that she wore when she used to read Bible stories to me at bedtime.

She told me the bad news, and I felt an awful sort of nothing inside me.

"The doctors gave me six months to live, son," she said softly.

"That can't be right, Mom," I muttered. "That can't be right."

"We just have to accept it, baby. I'm in God's hands now."

When I left her house that night, I looked up to the dark sky and cursed God out loud. As I wept, I thought about Jesus' final moments on earth, his broken body on a wooden cross in Golgotha.

I got in my truck and sped off to my apartment, blasting hip-hop on the radio the whole ride home.

Two months after my mother died, I got home from work one night depressed and beat to hell. If there was ever a time where I needed more sleep, I couldn't remember it. Without taking a shower or brushing my teeth, I collapsed into my bed and blacked out.

When I woke up in the middle of the night, there was a presence hovering above me. It looked like a meandering black storm cloud, blacker than anything I'd ever seen. One could say that my eyes were playing tricks on me, that my state of mind was in bad shape, and it was, but truth is, there was something there above me. It made the hairs on my arms stand up. It made my throat tighten up.

All of a sudden, I felt something long and pencil thin break through my lips and go into my mouth. It scraped the back of my throat, and I started to gag. I couldn't move, couldn't scream. All I could do was close my eyes and pray to Jesus out of habit.

As the situation was getting really bad, the thing went away. There was nothing in my mouth anymore. I opened my eyes, and the dark storm cloud was gone.

I felt a rush of joy so intense I wanted to cry. It was the same feeling I'd had after I caught a seventy-five-yard touchdown pass to help get the Mighty Warriors to the playoffs. It was a twice-in-a-lifetime kind of feeling.

The next day, after I mulled things over, I convinced myself that it had all been just a nightmare. But as time went on, I couldn't shake the feeling that the thing would come back for me, with its long and pencil-thin demonic straw. I could feel the straw breaking through my lips and going into my mouth. The back of my throat felt scratchy, and I knew exactly why. The more I thought about it, the more I was certain that it was only a matter of time before the thing would meander back into my room and finish the job.

One evening, I took a girl I was seeing to the local Dairy Queen for milkshakes. She ordered a strawberry one, and I a chocolate. I couldn't help but notice how she gripped her red straw and stirred her shake. She swirled the straw up and down and all around her cup.

I slurped my milkshake, and while it tasted great, the coldness irritated the back of my throat.

She continued to stir and sip, stir and sip, stir and sip. I started shaking my left leg nervously.

"Hey," I said, "I know this will probably come off wrong, so don't take offense, but can you please stop doing that?"

She looked at me with contempt.

"What, stirring my shake?" she asked, annoyed.

"Yeah. It's just ... It's kinda bothering me. Sorry."

That was pretty much the end of our relationship. It's the little things that are the hardest to recover from.

Long story short, what I'm getting at is it's been two years now since I've drunk a milkshake. Almost every day, when I drive by the Dairy Queen, I think about how I want nothing more than to sip on a chocolate shake in peace. I can almost taste its creamy, cold, sugary goodness melting on my tongue. But I haven't been able to bring myself to drink another one. I just can't. And I know the reason why, more or less. That's just the way it is.

Talk about torture.

Should've Just Stuck with the Damn Doritos

∞

The strangest thing anyone's ever told me was that I reminded them of a Ruffles sour cream and onion potato chip. That's right, a Ruffles sour cream and onion potato chip.

It happened my third year of college. A classmate—her name was Myra, and we'd had a few classes here and there—walked up to me after Ancient Religions one day and told me, with a smirk, "You know, you kinda remind me of a Ruffles sour cream and onion potato chip." Just like that.

Though I hardly knew Myra—an attractive girl who liked wearing loose-fitting stonewashed jeans—she never struck me as the type of person who said weird things just to say them. So basically, I was flabbergasted.

"Is that right?" I said, amused.

"Yep," she said cheerfully, then strutted away like it was no big deal telling me that I reminded her of a Ruffles sour cream and onion potato chip.

I must've stood in Myra's wake for a good while trying to digest her words.

Days flew by and I couldn't stop thinking about what she'd said to me. In between walking to class, sitting in the cafeteria, goofing off on my laptop, shooting hoops at the gym, and doing Lord knows what else, her comment buzzed around in my head like a housefly. Wherever I went, it followed. I decided I had to get to the bottom of it.

After a few days of hard thinking, I came up with a theory.

Myra, in her kindest way, was trying to tell me I was brackish! For starters, I wasn't a typical guy you find in college. I didn't go out drinking or clubbing with friends. Even just to eat out, I had to be bribed. I was a tightwad with my money in those days. In fact, I didn't have many friends. I was kind of a loner. But my theory had a critical flaw, and it was this: Myra wouldn't have known these particulars about me, exactly. We weren't close; we weren't in the same circles. Now, was it possible that she could've figured out I was this type of person by simply analyzing my face? Certainly. Other than a conversation-starting scar interestingly located above my left eyebrow, my face is rather plain, which is to say, reflective of a brackish personality. My nickname in middle school was Easter Island, after all. I was often told to loosen up. So perhaps, just maybe, Myra too was trying to tell me to loosen up, to straighten out my rough Ruffles ridges so to speak.

But why the hell a *sour cream and onion chip*, of all flavors? I wondered. I didn't have halitosis. I didn't reek of sour cream or onions. Hell, I didn't even like sour cream and onion potato chips all that much.

That question always stumped me. The one riddle I never solved.

It's been six years that I've been out of college now. I never mustered the courage to ask Myra what she ever meant. To do so now would require work. Too much work. Facebook stalking work. I'm not into that garbage, not at all. I've moved on. This ship has sailed.

Or so I thought.

A couple of months ago, my girlfriend Victoria was over at my place for dinner. We got to talking about our good old college days and, for whatever reason, I decided to bring up the Myra incident. It seemed a funny story to tell at the time. When I finished the story, Victoria's response was, "Weird." She said it stone-faced, like an Easter Island head.

"Everything okay?" I inquired.

"So, do you still talk to Myra?"

"Nope. Haven't seen her in six years."

"Hmm," she mumbled.

"What?"

"Nothing."

We finished our spaghetti in silence. After dinner, instead of cuddling with me on my couch like she usually did, Victoria said she was tired, that her stomach hurt and that she needed to go home.

"Want me to come with?" I asked.

"I'm good," she said, stone-faced.

Instead of asking her what was really wrong, which I already knew, I let her leave. I didn't want to get into it.

It occurred to me as she was leaving that Victoria was wearing stone-washed jeans. Something about Freud and the subconscious popped into my head, but I brushed that thought off like a gnat.

A few days later, while I was at the grocery store, I strolled through the chip aisle and stopped in my tracks when I saw a family-sized bag of Ruffles sour cream and onion chips. They were on sale: fifty cents off. Now, I didn't normally buy Ruffles; I didn't really like them. I'm a Doritos guy. Cool Ranch, if you want to know. But for whatever reason—maybe in perverse defiance, or maybe for no reason whatsoever—I bought that bag of Ruffles. They were on sale, after all. Fifty cents was fifty cents. Plus, I was long overdue to mix up my chips.

202 Alex Z. Salinas

The next day, Victoria was over watching TV with me. During a commercial break, she got up from my sofa and walked to the pantry to find something to munch on. Then, the next thing I knew, she was by my front door slipping on her sandals with a scowl on her face.

"Where're you going, Vickie-pants?" I asked.

"Home."

"What? Why?"

"Just because," she answered, stone-faced.

"What did I do now?"

"Nothing," she snapped.

I could've pressed the issue, but I wasn't in the mood, so I let her leave. She didn't slam the door, but she closed it hard enough. I heard a baby start to cry in the distance.

"For Heaven's sake," I said to myself.

A few minutes later, I went to my pantry.

I flicked on the light and noticed, smack-dab in the middle of the center shelf, the family-size bag of Ruffles sour cream and onion potato chips. I thought:

Should've just stuck with the damn Doritos.

Happy Enough

∞

Walmart doesn't pay the best but I'm happy working there. Happy enough. It's probably because I work a shitload of overtime and don't have student loans. Also Sally's low-maintenance and cool. She gives me foot massages and more just for bringing her fries and ice cream from McDonald's. It's literally the least I can do.

I moved out of my dad's right after high school. I'm 20 now so it's been 2 years. I've loved every second of it even with the bills. Sally too. We have an iguana named Paco. Sally named him that. Paco's all right.

My dad's a good dude just to be clear. When my mom died when I was 5 he took it hard. I remember him coming home from work and drinking beer until he cried into the sofa pillows. They'd be soaking wet. That was dad's routine for the longest. It was sad stuff. Anyway he really likes Sally but he didn't approve of her spending the night when I was at the house so I thought fuck it. When I graduate I'm moving out. So I did. And I'm happy.

One night after work not too long ago I hung out with some of the guys. My supervisor Ignacio was there. He's a good dude because he approves my overtime. He doesn't do that for everybody. After a while one of the guys pulled out a joint and lit it and passed it around. When it got to Ignacio he passed. Nobody said anything because he's Ignacio. When it got to me I also passed. They gave me shit but I didn't care. I wanted Ignacio to notice. As we were all leaving Ignacio walked with me to my truck. He said I made a smart move back there and asked if I was in school. I said naw. He said he went to college and it was all right but the only reason he was a supervisor was because of his college degree. In history. Fucking history. That's what he said.

When I got home Sally was asleep. I was off the next day. When I woke up I told Sally about my chat with Ignacio while she got ready for work. She knew where I was going before I finished. She cut me off and said if I wanted to go to college I better apply now and stop talking about it. Talking's for punk bitches she said. I looked at Paco and he was indifferent. Then I smiled and lifted Sally off the floor and kissed her all over.

I didn't know anything about applying to college so I went on Google and typed St. Jerome's. That's the college nearby. I read a little about St. Jerome's and got bored. I found the Apply Now button and clicked it. They wanted to know everything. There was a whole list of things. I scrolled down and saw they also wanted an essay. Jesus I thought. The question was what does freedom mean to me. Shit if I know. I've been out of school 2 years.

So I called my dad because I thought of Uncle Rudy. He'd been in prison since I was little for robbing a bank and shooting a cop. When my dad answered I told him about my application and asked if he was planning to visit Uncle Rudy anytime soon. My dad was thrilled I was going to apply to college but wanted to know what the hell Uncle Rudy had to do with anything. Long story I said. Are you visiting him or not. No he said. Okay I said and hung up.

If you want things done right you've got to do them yourself. So I went on Google and looked up the prison. I called the main line. Prisons have main lines. I learn something new every day.

In a nutshell they told me I had to book an appointment. They said I had to be put on a waiting list and be approved. But he's my uncle I said. It doesn't matter they said. Can't y'all expedite the process I said. Rules are rules they said. I learn something new every day.

So I thought YOLO and drove down to the prison. I walked right in and asked the front desk lady to see Uncle Rudy. You the guy I just talked to on the phone she said. What guy I said. Nevermind she said. Then she repeated the thing about the waiting list. Jesus is there a damn list for everything I said. She stared at me the way Paco did. I laughed.

Then get this. As I was leaving the prison some old dude approached me. He said he heard me mention a Rudy. He said he knew a Rudy. My uncle's name is Rudy I said. Rudy Villegas. That's him he said all excited. Rudy's a good man. A godly man. He said they used to read the Bible to other prisoners. It helped them sleep better at night. Wow I said. Perfect timing I thought. Then the old dude asked me what I was doing there. I told him about the essay and how if I wanted to know about freedom I should ask a prisoner. My uncle Rudy. Because he'd know. The dude grinned then wrote down his number on a piece of paper. He said call him later.

So I did. I called him again and again. He never answered. Not once. I didn't leave any voicemails. I didn't even know his name.

The whole thing pissed me off. I felt duped. Lied to. I didn't want to write essays or even see Uncle Rudy anymore.

I have a job and Sally. We have an apartment and a pet. I'm happy. We're happy enough. What more could I want. That's textbook freedom.

Maybe one day I'll email St. Jerome's a family photo of me and Sally and Paco. All of us smiling and free.

Burning of Non La

∞

Uncle Jerry carried the war like a scar. Slice open his tan barrel chest and you'd probably find the blood-soaked jungles beating inside.

One night, not long before he died, Uncle Jerry told me to fetch the old straw hat in his closet. He threw the hat in his fireplace and squirted lighter fluid on it.

He then told me to fetch jumbo marshmallows from his pantry.

We roasted them over the burning hat.

"Did you take the hat from a dead man?" I asked.

"An old friend," he answered.

We enjoyed the marshmallows in silence.

It was my first funeral.

Bare Hands

∞

Rogelio Alcocer, who'd had high blood pressure since his first chase of a woman at age fifteen, did not have, unlike his father, a violent temper. That may have all changed had Rogelio been a year older and drafted to Vietnam, witnessed the horrors of guerilla warfare and the scattering of limbs in the blood-soaked, Agent Orange-infested jungles, but fortunately Rogelio was spared that fate. Juan Antonio, Rogelio's father, wasn't so lucky. On the morning of July 27th, 1950, Juan Antonio was in Korea, stationed in the village of Hadong with the U.S. Army's 29th Infantry Regiment, when at 8:45 a.m., the North Koreans ambushed the regiment. They were on higher ground, in the mountains, and attacked Juan Antonio's unit from all angles, spraying them with gun fire and mortar. Juan Antonio's regiment, consisting mostly of new arrivals—acned young men with love notes stuffed in their pockets—lost almost its entire command staff in the first few minutes. The young soldiers retreated, digging foxholes and taking cover behind anything they could. The attack lasted two hours—an eternity. Juan Antonio witnessed dozens of his brothers-in-arms shot and blown to pieces. He would never unsee those images, never forget how when a person is shot, he doesn't fall down, but rather collapses awfully, as a marionette whose puppeteer is fed up and lets go of the handle. For the rest of his life, Juan Antonio would feel as if he was on borrowed time, riding on the backs of his lost brothers. Back at home, whenever things spun out of control, say a mouthy wife or a willful son who didn't seem to understand the meaning of respect, Juan Antonio's solution was simple: use swift force, teach them a hard lesson. Juan Antonio believed he needed to remind people to be thankful they hadn't seen what he'd seen, experienced what he'd experienced.

Rogelio lacked the animalistic switch his father could flick on instantly, but at age twelve, in Mrs. Lewis' English class, a boy sitting behind Rogelio stuck the tip of his eraser into Rogelio's ear and Rogelio snatched the eraser—nearly the boy's arm off, too—and threw the eraser across the classroom. Adult words, military language flew out of his mouth—phrases he'd picked up from his father. The boys and girls in the classroom shrieked and snickered. Mrs. Lewis grabbed Rogelio by his ear and dragged him to the principal's office. This was a story Rogelio enjoyed frequently telling, even the part where Juan Antonio punched him in his stomach as punishment. Rogelio was careful to clarify that his temper had not originated from his father, but rather from managing a bunch of kids at Whataburger when he was promoted to supervisor at the tender age of sixteen. Even then, Rogelio was broad-shouldered, wore a full Pancho Villa mustache. No wonder he commanded respect from his peers, young and old. Rogelio, it seemed, was practically born to manage people.

"Pops, how were you cool with Grandpa hitting you like that?" sixteen-year-old Troy asked Rogelio as they sat in the living room watching the Houston Astros get their butts handed to them by the Texas Rangers. Richie was with them, too, keeping quiet per usual.

"Had no choice," Rogelio answered, sipping Bud Lite from the bottle. "Times were different back then. We didn't question things, not like the way you kids do now."

"But still," Troy countered, "you didn't ever try to defend yourself? Hit Grandpa back?"

"No," Rogelio answered. "He was my father. I respected him. And that's why this country's going down the toilet. Because nobody has respect for anyone anymore."

An Astros player hit a homerun, a grand slam. They were back in the game. The announcers went crazy, the crowd wild.

Troy imagined that if his father ever hit him, he'd sock him right back—go for blood—and not give a damn about it.

"Pops, you really think things were better back then?"

Troy had asked his father this question many times, and his father's answer was usually yes. But every so often, Rogelio would rub his forehead, think a few seconds, then respond no, things weren't better back then.

Rogelio sipped his beer, rubbed his forehead.

"Yes and no," he answered this time. "Yes and no."

Richie stayed quiet, munching on potato chips, soaking it all in. When it came to his father, Richie preferred to play it safe.

. . .

One evening, when Troy was eight, Rogelio got home from work exhausted, his light-blue work shirt stained with oil, which meant a machine had broken down. All day long, Rogelio handled difficult personalities, most of them men, and sometimes he enjoyed it—but when it came to rolling up his sleeves, throwing himself into an old machine to locate and fix or to replace a part, it put a strain on his body, and later on he'd always feel it at home. A broken machine at the milk plant often required several hours of work to repair—hours of throwing yourself into tight spaces, reaching as far as you could into small crevices. This is the work required to produce America's milk, make its citizens' bones strong. Rogelio was not quite an old man, then—he could still tackle the physicality of his job—but he was no longer what his father called a spring chicken. His back, his knees ached increasingly.

When he got home from work—especially this evening, physically and mentally beat—all Rogelio wanted to do was crack open a beer and turn on the TV.

But this evening, what happened instead was Alma, his wife, intercepted him at the front door, not greeting him with her usual kiss; this time, she told her husband what had happened and demanded that he do something about their son. Rogelio sighed, rubbed his protruding brow ridge.

"I tell him again and again to get inside and he just ignores me," Alma said. "He doesn't listen."

Rogelio spotted Troy standing in the living room, a defiant look on his face.

"Then I sent Richie to get him but he pushed him," Alma said quietly, aware of Troy listening. "Richie bled all over the damn carpet. We just got that carpet installed."

Rogelio sighed again and rubbed his forehead. He figured a quick spanking was in order. Okay, he thought, one spanking and I'm calling it quits.

"This true, boy, what your mother's saying?" Rogelio asked Troy, still lurking in the living room.

Troy stared at his father, his lips pursed, his eyes filled with child anger. Rogelio recognized the glare well. He briefly recalled his father's reactions to his own outbursts—large fists slamming into his stomach. Rogelio's father had never asked confirmation questions; he just hit.

"I asked you a question, boy," Rogelio said louder.

Silence.

When Troy was a toddler, Rogelio prophesied that he would be a difficult child. Indeed, early on, Troy was temperamental, wanted to do things his way and on his terms. Rogelio possessed little patience for his first-born, and thus decided to start spanking him then, which often led to vicious tantrums. It was a cycle, but Rogelio, proud and stubborn, wasn't about to let his son rule his roost. However, Troy did have a tender side. Some days, he could be as kindhearted as his mother. Certain days, he could look you straight in the eyes with an understanding beyond his age. But most days, Troy's iron-willed gene dominated, and this inheritance from his father was one he could never return.

"Go to your room right now," Rogelio commanded.

Troy didn't budge.

"Now!"

Troy sped off, a frightened cat.

"Take it easy on him," Alma said, a drastic change in mood.

Rogelio gazed at Alma, pulled her close to him. He kissed her and said, "Of course I will, Almamacita."

Inside Troy's room, Rogelio told Troy to drop his pants, but to leave his underwear on. He knew soon, in the next year or so, this course of action would be inappropriate.

"You're getting three and we're done," Rogelio said, a judge sentencing his convict.

"Why you have to do this to me?" Troy protested. "None of my friends get spanked."

"I don't care about your friends."

"Their parents ground them. Why can't you ground me?"

"I decide what happens to you, boy."

"So stupid!"

"You're getting four spanks now and if you raise your voice at me one more time, you don't wanna know what's going to happen."

Troy grunted, the sound reminding Rogelio of an old tooth-less abuelita. He maintained a straight face.

After three, not four, spanks with his bare right hand—not hard spanks at all by his estimation—Rogelio left the room to let his son cool down. He heard Troy scream into his pillow, and Rogelio allowed this. If he didn't, he believed, there'd be trouble later on.

It usually took Troy twenty minutes or so to emerge from his room fully recovered. On this evening, only ten.

Troy found his father sitting in the kitchen, drinking Bud Lite from the bottle, his white-socked feet propped up on the dining table.

"You all right, boy?" Rogelio asked.

"Yeah," Troy mumbled.

"Good."

Father and son stared at each other for a couple seconds, then Rogelio asked, "Hungry?" He knew the answer would be yes.

"Yes," Troy muttered.

"Go get your brother and let's go to Whataburger."

Troy sped off, now an excited dog. Rogelio watched his son disappear. Gulped down the rest of his beer.

• • •

In college, Troy often swung by the Whataburger near campus, especially on Thursday nights after he and his roommates closed down the rec playing basketball. Whataburger was affordable, tasty, a classic choice. Plus, many of them stayed open 24/7.

One Thursday night, in the midst of guy-talk about girlfriends, crazy exes, grandiose business ideas, Troy almost shared with his roommates about how his father used to take him and his little brother to Whataburger after spankings. A sort of family tradition. He thought the guys might get a kick out of that.

But then Troy decided that some stories were meant to stay in the family.

• • •

It was June, scorching hot. Rogelio climbed the metal steps up to the rooftop. A bad hailstorm swept through San Antonio the day before, and the news said it was likely the costliest in city history.

Rogelio could've had one of his younger employees check the roof. The young guys always had the energy, something to prove, but Rogelio decided on this day to do it himself. Anyways, he thought, I need to burn off those breakfast tacos.

Rogelio walked around the rooftop snapping pictures from his work phone. There were holes in the silos, the damage significant. Rogelio whistled through his teeth and thought how this would be a huge dent on the budget.

Halfway coming down the metal steps, Rogelio belched, then felt a sharp tightness in his chest. He placed his hand over his heart as if to recite the pledge of allegiance. The tightness became stabbing, and Rogelio lost balance and barreled down the steps. A black curtain draped across his world.

Half an hour later, Kenny Chansombath, one of Rogelio's supervisors, found him collapsed on the steps.

"Ro!" screamed Kenny, rushing toward Rogelio.

He knelt down, put his hand in front of Rogelio's mouth, his nose. No air.

"OhmyGodohmyGod," Kenny said as he dialed 911.

When the EMTs arrived, Kenny watched them perform their jobs with rapid, precise movements—enough to inspire hope. But he noticed how their faces appeared as masks. Just another day on the job. Kenny wiped sweat from his forehead as he watched the EMTs work on his boss. He admired Rogelio, respected how he was direct and honest. He was a family man, Ro, always praising his wife and children. Ro was often politically incorrect, he'd bloviate how the Democrats were flushing the country down the toilet, but the milk plant wasn't a place for political correctness, and Ro was old-school anyways. He reminded Kenny of his own dad, who had died five years ago from a heart attack back in Laos.

Kenny wanted Rogelio to wake up so he could hug him, tell him he appreciated him, maybe even loved him. But when he saw he wasn't waking up, that the EMTs were wasting their efforts, he wanted to shout at them, "That's enough." But he was scared that if he tried to talk, no words would come out.

· · ·

The first thought that entered Troy's mind when he saw his father in the casket was the realization that he'd thought nothing at all. That his mind had been empty. You'd think something would've popped into his head, but no. Nothing.

Troy touched Rogelio's hand, which felt cold and waxy. Not human anymore. He tried reciting a prayer, but the words evaded him. A few seconds later, Alma placed her hand on top of Troy's. Troy looked at his mother and saw emptiness in her eyes. A shattered heart. It broke his own and he cried.

Richie, on the other side of Alma, hugged her, almost enveloping her. Alma buried her face in Richie's shoulder and wept. Though Richie wore a tweed jacket, he could feel the wetness seeping in. He rubbed his mother's back and prayed: Lord help us.

• • •

Troy was in his apartment, in bed, lights off, when the memory came to him.

He got up, went to the bathroom to urinate, wet his face. He washed his hands and examined himself in the mirror, his light brown eyes, wide shoulders.

The world beyond understanding, he thought. Existence a miracle, everything else a bonus.

Troy recalled his father's leathery hands. You earned every single one of those whoopings, he thought.

When I have kids, I'm going to whoop them too, and I'll let them throw their tantrums, and after they come find me, I'll ask them if they're all right, and after they say yes, and I say I love them, we'll go and celebrate.

Troy put on basketball shorts, a sleeveless shirt. He grabbed his car keys and hit the road. Almost 1 a.m.

He drove past McDonald's and almost turned around because he was whooped, but he pushed forward because otherwise it wouldn't feel right. Troy pinched his thigh.

He pulled into the drive-thru at Whataburger, squinted at the lit-up orange-and-white menu. He rolled down his window to accept the familiar greeting.

"Welcome to Whataburger, how can I help you?"

"One sec," Troy replied, eyeing the Number 1.

"All right, I think I'm ready."

"Go head."

"I need your help, actually."

"Oh-kay?"

"You see, a part of me really wants to order the kid's meal so I can get the toy that comes with it, but another part of me wants the Number 1. What'd you think? This is my dilemma."

"Uhhh."

After a few seconds of silence, the voice said, "That's up to you, man. That's your call."

Troy, smirking, couldn't believe what he was making happen right now.

"Look," he said, "I just need your recommendation. I won't go into all the details, but hypothetically speaking, if you were me, which option would you choose? The Number 1 or the kid's meal?"

More silence.

Poor guy, Troy thought, he probably thinks I'm gonna shoot up the place.

Finally, the voice responded, "Got kids?"

"Nope. Not yet at least."

"Well, I say you still go with the kid's meal. The toys we got are pretty freakin' awesome. They're these little spinny helicopter things. I was just playing with one before you pulled in, straight up."

Troy scratched his chin and said, "Spinny things, huh?"

"Yep, and if you buy two kid's meals you get two of them. Limited time only."

Limited time only, Troy thought. "You know what," he said, an idea coming to his mind, "let's make that three kid's meals, kind sir."

. . .

Richie got home from the gym, his gray Under Armour shirt almost black from sweat. He threw all of his mail on his kitchen counter except for a cardboard envelope labeled Priority Mail. He ripped it open and reached inside, retrieved a small object wrapped in clear plastic. It was painted dark blue and had a ball bearing in the center where attached there was a propeller. Richie wasn't sure what to think, but he thought it looked like a toy that came from a fast-food restaurant. Something else was inside the envelope.

The note said, in red capital letters: *LOVE, POPS.*

Richie stared at the note in awe and disbelief. The script

looked exactly like his father's—sloppy, all caps. Quite unbe-
lievable.

Richie brought the plastic-wrapped toy to his nose and
sniffed. The scent faint, but unmistakable: French fries.

He sat on his couch and felt his whole body sink into it, as if
he weighed one thousand pounds.

Richie had believed in God his entire life. Before his father
had died, he'd attended mass most Sundays, chatted with
friends about the goodness of the Lord, even encouraged
some of them to go with him, especially girls he was trying to
date. Because of his good listening, a few of Richie's friends
confided in him certain hardships of their lives: breakups,
drug and alcohol addictions, money problems, family
secrets, and in the case of one young woman, the death of her
father, which spawned her depression. In those days, which
weren't long ago, Richie seemed to have all the free advice
in the world, but not so anymore. He went to work, worked
out, went out, drank, sometimes slept around, went home,
and drank some more. The other night, he downed a whole
bottle of whiskey. Vomited his guts out, called in to work.
Each morning, facing his latest self in the mirror, Richie realized he'd been all talk. Hot air. The Hindenburg. He ignored
calls from his friends and sometimes from his own mother,
though he couldn't say why. The only person he talked to on
occasion was Troy.

Staring at the note, Richie traced the handwriting with his
thumb. Eyes closed, he clutched the toy, trying to crush it. If
anything, maybe it'd melt to goo in his hand. But in reality,

he wanted there to be nothing in his hand. He wanted to open his eyes and find the world as it had been.

He loosened his grip. The plastic wrap crumpled, warm and slick with moisture.

Richie walked to his kitchen, opened the cupboard, pulled out a glass and a bottle of Wild Turkey. Filled the glass to the brim, swooshed the dark liquid around and around, tasting the burn before it was.

He couldn't hear his cell phone buzzing because he hadn't realized it'd slipped out of his shorts and into his couch cushions. If Richie had had his phone on him, he would've taken his brother's call. Would've been asked if he'd checked the mail, and the conversation that followed, the laughs, probably would've relieved his mind off that first drink.

Rainbow
Suspenders

∞

Mr. Hurley would wander around the McDonald's.

In daylight, he'd repeat Jesus' parables to passing customers.

At night, he'd ask for whatever could be spared—fries from the dollar menu would be okay.

I went there every Friday. I once made the mistake of making eye contact with him.

"When ya get a lil' older, buy me a Big Mac, kid," he said, flashing his green-brown teeth.

A couple of years later, he was found dead against the church entrance, clutching the strap of his signature rainbow suspenders.

I cried when it happened.

I would've eventually bought him a Big Mac.

Santa Always Blows His Cover

∞

It was Christmas 1995 when Mom burnt the bacon and Dad was just getting home. I tore open the packaging to the Mortal Kombat-brand plastic ship and Ray pulled a puppy out of a box.

"Ruby!" he announced, holding up the furry dog he'd dreamt of since summer.

"Where's Liu Kang and Raiden?" I asked out loud, the question meant for Mom. For a child on Christmas day, what are toy vehicles without action figures to steer them?

"Your mom shopped around everywhere for that thing, so knock it off," Dad answered in his oil-stained uniform. "Now let's eat."

After breakfast—about forty-five pancakes Mom had stirred up for us since she fed us like linebackers—we were corralled to the garage where there were two new bicycles, mine Scorpion-yellow, Ray's Reptile-green.

Fifteen seconds later Ray crashed into the oak tree in our front yard. He came away with scraped knees, a split lip, the indignity of knowing that the next-door neighbor girls had watched him cry.

I was older than him by three years, so I stayed outside riding in circles, round and round, wheee! I showed off the training I'd received from my best friend, Jordan, who was white, so of course that fool had had a bike since the age of negative one.

The thing about Christmas, for the longest time, was how Mom always burnt the bacon and how now, no one's around to do it, so I burn my own. I know my wife hates it, barely tolerates it, but she understands the fragile thread that's there. The smell.

Ray and I send each other $50 gift cards every year. We believe it an even exchange, efficiency at its finest, although last December I texted him what's the point if in the end there's a zero balance.

"Good point," he responded. Followed by a thumbs-up emoji. A shrugging-man emoji.

I know he gets torn up about the holidays the same way as I do, Ray, but this year I'll send him $100. Surprise him.

He'll spend the extra dough on booze, maybe new shoes,

videogames. Most likely he'll save some of it. His wife manages their budget.

And then in a few months, probably in March, when the sun starts frying us, I'll wonder to myself during a quiet stroll, Hey, man, why the hell didn't you just buy him a plane ticket? Invite 'em over. It's the least you could've done, you cheap, lazy bastard. Mom and Dad would be *so* proud of you right now. So proud.

Maybe next year. Yeah, definitely next year.

Plenty of Time

∞

Today I heard the wailing of ambulance sirens in the shower. I rushed washing myself and shivered into clothes, sped to Midas to have my car inspected only to discover my insurance card expired six months prior.

I'm thirty-two—a prime but informative existence. Mortality upgraded from acquaintanceship to booty calls. She too hits me up now whenever she wants—sundown, sunrise. (Why a she? Because I'm childless.)

Last week I awoke, commenced the routine of brushing my teeth only to find in my grip my razor.

There's still plenty of time to giggle about these things. (A frightening word, giggle.)

The Interview

∞

The elevator hummed and I was annoyed as hell. The bright hot lights had my brows dripping, armpits swampy. Anything stronger than forty watts and it was as though I was being slow-cooked inside a Croc-Pot. I've always hated the light. My earliest memory—a dream?: a man shining a flashlight, a lantern, in my face. In my mind's eye, I can never make out his features; he's always just out of focus. Perhaps he's my father. I remember the deep, cold terror—the kind that thins your blood permanently as a kid. I thank that memory (a dream?) for encouraging me to find comfort in the dark, to hug the shadows. In second grade, I nicknamed my shadow Seal, after the singer. *I've been kissed by a rose on the gray*. Back then I'd hide in my closet for what seemed hours, lying down, stretched out like a cat whether sleep arrived or not. My mom said it was because I was born at midnight, on Friday the 13th, during monsoon season, that God made me the man I am.

All over my blue Calvin Klein suit, dust—layer upon layer of flimsy shards of me.

Jesus, I thought, next time you leave the house be sure to open your eyes.

Then again, all the windows in my apartment are draped with brown bedsheets. My roommate—my uncle Juan—prefers natural light, says the sun gives his skin a desirable bronze glow. Ever the ladies' man, my uncle Juan. He complains about my makeshift curtains, sure, but he also understands that I pay the bills, therefore I decide our lighting situation, or lack thereof.

I patted down my suit, shook my coat sleeves. Dust floated everywhere, gross and hilarious, as if for ages my body had been stored away then suddenly taken out, put on display. A seasonal museum exhibit.

I couldn't recall the last time I'd worn a suit. Had I ever worn one other than for my First Communion? I never dressed up for work. My station was in a tiny cubicle in the corner of a small office in the corner of an old building. There was a restroom on the other side of my wall and often I dreamt about flushing toilets. *Whoosh!*

The elevator stopped on floor six. I straightened up. The doors opened. Nobody was there—just a brightly lit hallway at the far end of which hung, slightly crooked, a print of Van Gogh's "Starry Night." A typical selection, but hardly in poor taste.

I walked down the hall squinting stupidly like a B-level Clint Eastwood. The heat through the ceiling panel lights are frying me, I thought. Suddenly I had a hankering for an egg sandwich.

I stood in front of Suite No. 623. Before stepping inside, I asked myself how I'd gotten there—the elevator, the office, my hand resting on the cold metal handle.

Idiot, you drove in your car, I thought. But that can't be right because today you rode the bus for the first time ever. But no, what about the sad-looking brunette on the subway, wretched and beautiful? She was a dream, but no way could you make her up. Idiot, you're fixing to be late.

I opened the door and behind a huge oak desk, there she was, smiling. Twentysomething, hardly any makeup, snug green dress exposing her curves like hatchlings. I could hardly believe the evidence, but everything considered, I had zero say in the matter.

"Mr. Mendax?" she inquired, her eyes cheerful and expectant.

"Speaking," I answered, suddenly filled with brimming confidence like that of a hardboiled detective.

"Glad you made it! Your interviewers were called into an emergency meeting a few minutes ago, but it shouldn't take much longer. Please have a seat and I'll call you as soon as they're ready."

I checked my watch, though I already knew I was fourteen minutes early. I moseyed over to the sofa beside the receptionist's desk, on the verge of asking her if she'd remembered me on the train. I bit my tongue and plopped down, my muscles loosening instantly.

"The battle's practically won," I murmured to myself. "Seventy-five percent was getting your tushy here."

My heartrate slowed to a crawl. With a clearer head I inspected my fingernails—a healthy pink, freshly clipped. I reexamined my suit—clean as a Calvin Klein whistle.

The receptionist's phone rang and in the span of a blink she answered it.

Just as soon I'd already decided she was a 9.75 out of 10, especially now that she appeared happier, with vigor and purpose. As a rule, I never dished out perfect 10's to strangers, but people got close.

"Bobby," she answered, her cheeks blushing.

The beau. Go figure, I thought. I assumed Bobby was in medical school. He had red curly hair, was tall and handsome, athletic too. In high school, he played starting quarterback, and everything about him, from the manner in which he walked—strutted, really—chest puffed out, human Clydesdale—to the way he talked told you everything you needed to know. His patented twinkle in his blue-green eyes broke down the defenses of any cheerleader in his path much in the same way he broke down the pre-strategized defenses of his opponents on the gridiron, picking 'em apart with his gunslinging cannon. But for Bobby, this otherwise shining knight, there was a chink in his armor: *he was vain as shit.* Because despite enjoying a breezy, suburban life devoid of hardship thanks to his dough-machine parents, Dr. Robert (an orthodontist, which explained Bobby's perfect teeth, though they were a little on the large side, like a Clydesdale's), and Sheryl (a lawyer who went by Sherri with an "i"), Bobby was ultimately ill-trained in the fine art of wholesome bonding—in other words, incapable of allowing his gorgeous receptionist girlfriend to feel truly secure in their relationship. This is the affliction of all leading men who don't work hard for their women. Bobby had lots of friends—girl friends, that is, with a separation between the nouns. He'd always had them, his girl friends—nothing new to report here. They'd flocked to him since he could remember, the suckers, but really, what could Bobby say? He liked the attention, adored it big time. In one way or another, Bobby was always engaged in conversation with members of his flock, the list of which included Sara, Tanya, Vanessa and Maria; basically any female whose name ended in "a." Let's not forget Lisa, the chick who Bobby and Gorgeous Receptionist ran into that one time at Starbucks. If you'd've asked Gorgeous then, she'd've said Lisa was a little too friendly the way she hugged Bobby, rubbed her pretty little manicured fingers all around his broad back. She'd crossed the thread-thin tumultuous border, Lisa had (according to Gorgeous), between the Friend Zone and the Bone Zone. When Bobby's phone lit up at all times of day and night—Gorgeous had come to think of his ever-glowing device as possessed—and when he'd read his text messages and grin—that patented twinkle in his blue-green eyes—Gorgeous would wonder. One day, she asked him, "Who're you always texting?" "Friends," Bobby answered drily. "Just friends." Right. Sure. Uh-huh. Another day, when Gorgeous was, how can I word this delicately ... enduring her monthly trial ... she asked Bobby, "Bobby, why are so many of your friends girls?" Gorgeous was conscientious of her tone as to not come across as accusatory; she'd simply asked a question, one that could theoretically be answered in good faith. Bobby was silent for a few seconds, seemingly taken aback, and in those few seconds of no reply, Gorgeous noticed that Bobby's face twitched subtly, in an ugly way that transformed his visage wholly, granting him the probability of possessing real flesh that could flatten over time, betray its owner if stabbed over and over with grooming scissors. Finally, Bobby answered Gorgeous in a tone concealing no condescension whatsoever, almost firing a question back at her: "Because there are more women than men on Earth?" To which he immediately followed up with, "And why do you wanna know anyways?" This, of course, was his critical error. The great crack down the center of his mask. His façade. As days passed by, as blue morning skies melted into pitch-black nights, a thought manifested—grew and spread disease-like—in Gorgeous' impacted mind. In one week's span, the thought—nay, the premonition, the certainty—was it would only be a matter of time before the tall drink of water whose Christian name was Robert, better known as Bobby, who in the future would be known professionally as Dr. Rob, would leave her high and dry for *someone else.* Suddenly it mattered not one iota that Bobby would someday reel in the big bucks, be able to buy her an engagement ring the size of a baby hippo. It didn't matter that he'd someday be capable of gifting her a dreamy honeymoon to Malta—it was either there or Greece, but everybody and their mom went to Greece. It didn't matter that he'd someday provide her with a six-bedroom house in a gated community where chubby gate guards sat around pretending they were real police. While these ruminations all sounded great on paper, none of them mattered because they were all of the material world, and if there was one thing Bobby should've known about Gorgeous, it was that she sure as hell wasn't one of those kinds of girls. So, after a few evening calls with Stacy, Gorgeous' best friend since elementary, who'd helped Gorgeous arrive at a decision, a decision she eventually knew was the correct one for spiritual salvation—for she believed in concepts such as the soul, which, mind you, Bobby did not, despite his Catholic upbringing—Gorgeous convinced herself alas that she'd be all right without Bobby. After all, deep down in her heart, she knew she was a 9.75 out of 10, and 9.75's never stay physically lonely for very long. It was a Friday night at Baskin-Robbins. Gorgeous let Bobby pay for her ice cream. After half an hour of small talk (which she would later come to think of as tiny talk), and with a half-full stomach, she finally piped up to the ex-before-her-eyes, "Bobby, I have something I need to tell you. I don't think we're going to work out." Immediately upon registering her simple declarative, Bobby's jaw dropped slightly open, and from out of his mouth dribbled Burgundy Cherry ice cream. For the first time in his breezy life, Bobby felt a stabbing pain—a plunge through his soul. (Yes, the soul was real, he could now attest.) It hurt—hurt like a motherfucking spear tackle from behind. He knew the pain was just beginning, would last a long, long time. Fast forward as Dr. Rob readied himself for bed, positioning himself just right on his brand-new Tempur-Pedic mattress, taking in the silky-softness of a one-thousand-thread-count bed sheet (the very best that Bed Bath & Beyond had to offer).

Out of nowhere—as most things in life occur—her words returned to him again. And each time they reappeared they echoed a little louder. *I don't think we're going to work out.* Dr. Rob peered down at his trim housewife, Lisa, who was peacefully asleep. Be still my heart, he thought tenderly. He wondered then out of pure curiosity, Am I really happy? *Of course I am*, he reassured himself, *of course I'm happy*. He thought of his two boys, Riley and Jacob, who were also fast asleep in their bunk beds. Ah, Riley and Jacob, the WASPiest little rascals you always hear about. Xboxes and PlayStations and the latest Jordans. *I'm blessed*, Dr. Rob thought, *truly and eternally blessed. Thank you, Lord. Amen.* He lowered his head onto his pillow, closed his eyes, imagined himself unplugging his highly trained brain from the earth. But before sleep would knock him out, he'd be confronted by a final, nasty illusion in the form of ghostly words: *It should've been* HER *sleeping next to me right now*. Dr. Rob replayed how swiftly she had slipped from his grasp, as though she'd been a football from the gods he could never fully grip, spiraling into a labyrinthine locker room, spinning, spinning, spinning, gone, gone, gone ....

"Mr. Mendax, they're ready for you now," the receptionist announced.

Startled, I leapt from the sofa.

"Follow me, please."

"You got it, Gorgeous," I said without thinking.

"Beg your pardon?"

"Um—nothing."

As I followed behind her down a narrow corridor, leaving a few steps of distance between us out of mild embarrassment, I went over some answers to hypothetical questions.

Hypothetical Question Number One: What is it about our publishing house that interests you?

Hypothetical Answer Number One: Great question. Your house carries a long tradition of excellence in putting out superior work. Your reputation for being forward-thinking, economically stable and engaged in the community, such as the recent oil cleanup y'all helped with, precedes you. I'd love to be part of your team, and with my editorial experience, I believe I'd fit right in.

Hypothetical Question Number Two: What would you say is your biggest strength?

Hypothetical Answer Number Two: I consider myself a life-long learner—I'm always trying to learn something new every day—but if I had to pin down my biggest strength, I'd say it's that I'm a hard worker. Once I set my mind to doing something, I get it done no matter what. I guess you can say working too hard is also my biggest weakness.

Hypothetical Question Number Three: May you elaborate on that?

Hypothetical Answer Number Three: Of course. I've been told many times by my supervisors and colleagues that I ought to take more breathers. "Enjoy life, you can't work hard all the time," they say to me. "I do enjoy life," I tell them, "but that includes hard work."

Hypothetical Employer Comment: Quite impressive!

Hypothetical Response to Hypothetical Employer Comment: Oh, it's nothing.

In front of me, a small room lit exclusively by a green banker's lamp, lending the space a tavernous vibe as if I was joining in on a séance. At the center of the room, behind another huge desk, sat a black-haired woman, and in the back corner leaning against the wall, a bald man in a suit with large sunglasses à la someone straight out of *Men in Black*.

The woman's face was cast in soft glow, and in front of her was a manila folder.

"Mr. Mendax, pleasure to meet you," she said, offering me her hand from the shadows, her fingernails painted oddly some shade of yellow. Her bones felt slender in my grip.

"I hope you don't mind the lighting," she said politely.

"Not at all, Miss ...?"

"Leena. Leena Veritas."

"Veritas," I said, feeling an old foreign weight escape my lips.

With her dark hair, thick jet-black streaks for eyebrows, Leena looked exactly like Jennifer Connelly—Jennifer Connelly's twin sister born somewhere far and cold. In Soviet Russia.

"The guy in the corner there is Mr. Vulcan, Lee Vulcan," said Leena with an air of amusement. "He's here for quality assurance purposes, so rest assured he isn't Dracula in disguise."

I waved at him, but he stood motionless, his face an oblique blank covered with ridiculously large sunglasses.

Inside my chest, a sudden event: tribal beats vibrating up my rib cage.

Leena hit me with a question, to which I answered:

"Yes ma'am, everything's fine. But to be honest, I had some trouble sleeping last night."

"Completely understood," Leena said. "I never seem to get enough sleep myself. I'm convinced it's something to do with my phone. Modern-day struggles and all."

"Phones're bad for the mind," I confirmed. "But then again, maybe the lighting in here."

Leena's laugh was quick, warm.

"Yes," she agreed. "I do feel more, I don't know, alive in the dark, as unprofessional as some may find that outlook."

To Leena's left I spotted a small print tacked on the wall, placed it immediately: Edward Hopper's "Rooms by the Sea."

Back in college I took two art history classes, one of them being Contemporary American Art. For my final paper, I remember poring over Edward Hopper's work, came to enjoy his fabricated evenings, his dusky twilights. I'd read that Hopper was a dour introvert—not the kind of dude you'd bring around guests at a dinner party. His wife, Josephine, also an artist, was Hopper's polar opposite, temperamentally speaking. As her husband's reputation grew, her's shrunk, and yet their marriage still lasted forty-three years. I believe I also read that Hopper would sometimes beat on Jo. Poor Jo. The better and abused half of a great man.

"Ed Hopper, huh?" I said to Leena.

"Yep," answered a voice from the back corner. "A boring piece if you ask me."

Suddenly I got the revolting sense I'd been incapable of reading the room—I was in cahoots with dangerous players.

"He's one of my favorites," I countered dismissively, a shot in the dark, literally.

Mr. Vulcan retorted with something about Hopper's inability to capture objects precisely as they appear, which, in his opinion, was the only mark of an artist's genius.

"Unlike the masterful Norman Rockwell, the prince of America," said Mr. Vulcan flatly.

"Quality art," I rebutted, "is obviously predicated on subjectivity. I question anyone who believes in his heart there's a single set of standards determining what's good and bad."

Immediately I thought: God, I sound like doofus, I sound like I look exactly like one of those liberal arts doofuses on college brochures. Then I thought: It's his stupid sunglasses. Those ridiculous sunglasses in the dark.

"Speaking of heart," Mr. Vulcan said, "in case you're wondering, I'm blind as a bat, son."

My face was hot. Then Leena broke in gently, but firmly. "Mr. Mendax, while I'm enjoying our conversation, we respect your time, so I suggest we begin your interview.

"If there's time afterward, you and Mr. Vulcan are more than welcome to resume your discussion."

She opened the manila folder, cleared her throat, smiled. Smooth as cream in our little chambers.

"Judging from your résumé, it's clear you have lots of experience in publishing. You worked for Rollins and Jones, and also for Davis and McPhearson, is that correct?"

"Correct," I said, moving right along. "I was at Rollins and Jones for two years, and Davis and McPhearson for another two. I was also at Johnson and Anderson but only for six months—that was before Rollins hired me."

"Impressive," Leena said. "Respectable shops—our competitors, naturally, but very good. So what interests you in our house?"

I breathed in deeply, exhaled, just as rehearsed.

"Great question, Leena. Let me start by saying that your house carries a long tradition of excellence in producing superior work. Your reputation for being forward-thinking, economically stable and engaged with the community, such as the recent oil cleanup y'all pitched in with, precedes you. With my editorial experience, I believe I'd fit right into your team."

Leena scribbled down a few notes on a legal pad. Mr. Vulcan loomed silent, arms crossed.

"So, Mr. Mendax, what would you say is your biggest strength as an employee?"

I nodded, allowed her question to linger a moment, precisely as planned.

"Great question, Leena. Well, I do consider myself a lifelong learner—I'm always trying to learn something new every day—but if I had to pin down my biggest strength, I'd say it's that I'm a hard worker. Once I set my mind to doing something, I get it done no matter what. I suppose you can say working too hard is also my biggest weakness."

Leena jotted down more notes, then replied, "May you elaborate, please?"

"Of course. I've been told on several occasions by my supervisors and colleagues that I need to take more breathers. 'Enjoy life, you can't be working like crazy all the time,' they say to me. 'I do enjoy life,' I tell them, 'but that includes hard work.'"

I noticed crow's feet form around Leena's eyes; the white glow of her teeth indicated I'd strung together a proper combination of sentences.

"Impressive," she said.

I smiled, shrugged. I thought: What would the pope do right now? He'd tell the masses what they need to hear.

While a thunderstorm was howling outside, I felt cozier now that I'd begun talking my lines. Leena watched me with sustained interest.

"Mr. Mendax, it's refreshing to hear that you like to go to work. Rest assured, you're in the right place for that, then. But I must say, we do run rather aggressive operations. A tight ship, if you will. We're extremely selective in who we pick. On average, our employees log fifty-hour work weeks. Is that something you might've heard about us already?"

"That won't be an issue," I said, digging my toes into my worn leather shoes.

"We work with lots of demanding clients on often very short deadlines," Leena continued. "If you don't pace yourself, you'll find that's it very easy to drown here. But we also cultivate a team environment, relying on each other to pick up the slack when necessary. That said, our pay's highly competitive. On our facility, we have a gym, a swimming pool, a Jacuzzi and multiple basketball and tennis courts. We hire personal trainers for employees. As you mentioned earlier, we're forward-thinking. We also offer educational benefits that take affect after six months of employment. If you're thinking about grad school, well, we've got you covered. Did I mention we have excellent health insurance plans?"

Leena punctuated her elaborations with friendly hand gestures. She was matronly, almost.

"Your references check out. Actually, they all said amazing things about you." She flipped through the pages of my application. "Things're looking on the up and up."

I momentarily imagined sliding down a mound of extra income, this cash dangling before me like a piece of medium-rare steak.

"If I may, there is one thing I'm curious about, something I need to address. You mind if I ask you a personal question regarding your work history?"

"Not at all," I lied.

"There seems to be a—how to put this—a two-year pattern of you working and then subsequently departing to somewhere else. Now I'm sure there's sensible explanation for that, and really, it's none of my business—but to be completely honest, the most essential thing we value in our associates is stability. Loyalty we view as gold, which is the reason we've been extraordinarily successful. Do you see what I'm getting at, Mr. Mendax?"

"Absolutely," I said.

I met Leena's gaze, her inspection, as though she were the Mona Lisa and I a regular patron. I'd thoroughly prepared for this. And thus, like Mona Lisa, she smiled slyly, said, "Wonderful."

Discreetly I surveyed the room, realizing with the horror of a few seconds the absence of Mr. Vulcan. There was only one door into the office—one way in, one way out. There was no way I would've missed him leaving.

"Excuse me, Leena, but where did Mr. Vulcan—"

"Mr. Mendax, let me ask you, are you an honest person?"

"What?" I said.

"I said, are you an honest person."

Her question forced my attention on her, which is how I noticed her hair was no longer in a bun—her hair curly, thick and wild. She seemed to occupy more space, as if everything in the cramped room revolved around her, the sun at the center of our solar system. A brutish dwarf of a star.

"I'm sorry, you were saying," Leena said.

"Y-yes," I stammered.

Then, following a quick breath, I said with all the gravity I could muster:

"Leena, you will tell me where Mr. Vul—"

The heat exploded in my ears. I jumped out of my seat but was yanked down hard, my wrists strapped to the chair.

First the buzzing of flies then the smell of rotting animals. The heat returned, and it was pure and awful, and I screamed.

"Now now, be a good little doggy," Mr. Vulcan said from behind me, plucking his fingers from my ears.

Again I launched but the stopped motion jerked me in place, pinched my back. All I could think about was squeezing his neck, watching him die between my hands.

"If you don't cool it, Mr. Mendax, I'm afraid Mr. Vulcan'll be forced to see just how far his fingers can go in.

"Now listen carefully," she said coldly. "You knew we'd be waiting for you. You knew what was going to happen today. You knew once you crossed the Valley of Death, you'd sacrifice your double heart."

"Let me go," I pleaded. "Let go. Forget all this."

I tried looking away but he pressed me at the temples, dug his fingernails into my eyelids.

"You think your mother would be proud of you, Mr. Mendax? Your poor uncle?"

Before I could speak he slammed two knives in my chest, buried down to the hilts.

"A blade for each," he said.

There was no blood, but when my eyes closed I felt it spill out.

Somebody whispered in my ear.

Couldn't understand. Heard nothing.

• • •

An empty studio, plain white walls.

Daylight, whip of crashing waves.

"Wanna go for a swim?" Uncle Juan says. "It's nice out. Yer momma's already there."

"There?" I say.

"Let's get a move on, chump."

The green water, cloudless blue sky. Cry of seagulls.

A figure in the distance. Woman on water.

Raises her arms; from above, white roses raining down. Down I look; blood dyeing the ocean.

The sea, a red cotton field. A titan's candy cane.

• • •

Trooper wakes me with his long slimy tongue down my throat.

"Jesus! I'm up!"

I hop out of bed and there's a slight tremor in my legs, my legs feeling like soggy toothpicks. The hazy light poking through the blinds tells me it's midmorning, roughly. People up and moving.

In the bathroom mirror I spot a red angry bump on the tip of my nose. With bags under my eyes, cowlicks on both sides of my head, I feel as near as possible to my homely self-image.

I splash water on my face, brush my teeth, floss.

Trooper's parked next to me, panting, tail wagging, big dog smirk.

"But you don't really love me," I say to our golden retriever.

I open the drawer under the sink, grab from a container a handful of treats, hold them above Trooper's snout. He goes berserk, spins four or five times, then sits, homed in on my fist.

"But you don't really love me, do you, Troop? I'm just your sugar daddy."

At my teasing he yelps, then I drop his treats. I'm about to head to the living room but something compels me—call it the Creative Impulsive—to halt mid-foot-lift. I go to my laptop, open it, sit on the floor and type out my dream, sequence by sequence. It's the first time I've transcribed a dream. (Bad luck?) I convince myself it's practice to improve my skills. Halfway through the exercise, about five pages in, I question how much of it's already exaggerated, stretched, clued in by a woken brain.

Uncle Juan's on the sofa, breathing heavy, TV turned on to CNN or FOX. He's wearing a black muscle shirt, gray sweatpants. He's wrapped up his daily pushups.

"Mornin', chump," he greets me.

"Morning. What time is it?"

"Time to get a new watch," he says. "Naw, it's eleven. Somebody slept like a princess."

"Pretty rough, yeah."

"Welp, spill the beans, dude. How'd it go?"

"How'd what go?"

"Uh, your interview, Einstein."

"Oh, yeah."

My hand rubs around my chest automatically.

"Man ... it's hard to say."

Uncle Juan studies me briefly, then he says:

"Tanked it, huh?"

I'm quiet—my mind replaying the graphic narrative I'd cemented, the images of which are seeming to disassociate from memory. (A dream?)

"Check it out, chump," my uncle says, sitting up straight on the edge of our sofa. "If there's anyone who knows about tanking, it's moi. Let me tell ya, I've mastered the art of tanking. I've got a master's degree in it—no, shit, a Ph.D. But yer still young, so the way I see it is, you gotta keep going out there, do what needs doing, over and over till the walls of Jericho come crashing down hard. Feel me? Word?"

He shadow-boxes the air, an invisible opponent, unleashing a mean combination of jabs and uppercuts.

"Word," I repeat.

On the TV, a blonde anchor with humongous eyes reports on a domestic violence incident from last night involving a young couple with a baby—ingredients for half of all campfire stories. The boyfriend shot her, and now she's in the hospital in critical; the baby's healthy and doing fine. A mugshot of the thug: young, Hispanic, shaved head, tattoos creeping up his needle neck.

"How can you stomach this crap?" I say.

"Gotta stay informed. Gotta be in the know." Uncle Juan taps his forehead.

"You belong on the news," I say, instantly regretting it.

"Been there, done that."

The broadcast goes to commercials and without a hitch my uncle hops back on his pedestal.

"Seriously, dude, you'll find something better, keep trucking along. Yer a smart guy, being my bloodline and all. Word?"

"Word," I repeat.

"And once you get them celeb stacks, sheeit, the chicas'll be all over your ass, way hotter than that last one—whatsher-name again?"

"Tiffany."

"The Tiffster! Man, ballbuster, that chick. What kinda name's Tiffany anyway? White people, dude. White people. Mayonnaise and hummus."

The blonde anchor returns with another breaking story: a married politician caught paying for prostitutes using tax-payers' money. (How dare he!)

The news cycles: barrages, labyrinths of trash. Endless and endlessly unchanging, like everything else. I want to tell my uncle my dream, but I know there'd be no point in doing so. On the other hand, I can't update him about the interview because there's not much to report on that front, not really. Everything's fuzzy. So I ask him instead:

"Doing good on money?"

"Yeah, 'nuff for groceries."

"Still no bites?"

"Naw. Filled out some more applications yesterday, but we'll see how it goes. Maybe Mickey D's'll call me back."

One night a few years ago, Uncle Juan, drunk, hit an old lady walking across the street. She was carting groceries back to her home, where her bedridden husband was waiting for her, worried that his wife still went out by herself. In his state of disorder, Uncle Juan didn't see her, and the impact from the accident broke her legs and pelvis. A week later she died in the hospital. They discovered Uncle Juan had been driving with a blood-alcohol content level of .20. When they informed him that the old woman had died, it was in that instant, he told me later, that a piece of him died too. "You think God'll forgive me?" he asked me when I went to visit him. "Of course," I said, although the truth was, how could I know the answer to that question? When Uncle Juan's trial came around, the judge—the Honorable Jerry Ordo—told him, with six people present in court including myself and five family members of the deceased Mrs. Graciela Esperanza, that he was considering sentencing him to ten years because DUI manslaughter wasn't something to wash your hands of. Judge Ordo said a precious life had been needlessly taken—a fine lady, a wife, a mother, a loving grandmother—due to my uncle's stupid decision, a fatal lapse in judgment. You should thank the Lord, Ordo said to Uncle Juan, that you didn't get yourself killed too. He laid into him a few minutes more, then revealed the silver lining: Uncle Juan had served a tour in the Army during Desert Storm, was honorably discharged with a Purple Heart and a Silver Star, earned by escorting eight Kuwaiti villagers to safety in the face of gunfire. Uncle Juan took a 9mm bullet to his thigh, but with his adrenaline pumping, he completed the task of getting the villagers to safety. Luckily for us, Judge Ordo too had served in Desert Storm, himself as an Air Force captain. Ordo, despite my uncle's predicament, in spite of himself, had a soft spot for him, for the judge admitted he knew all too well the psychological damage that war inflicts on man. He understood all too well how it drives men to the bottle, and to worse. Uncle Juan didn't have a previous criminal record, only a record of job-hopping after his discharge, the last of which was dayshift supervisor at Walgreens. Ordo said to my uncle that if he played his cards right, he could be free in four years. I expect excellent behavior from you, hero, he said, and if you let me down, I'll personally kick your ass and throw away the key. As he said this, he smiled painfully. This isn't the end for you, Juan, Judge Ordo said. Redemption starts for you today. Right this second. He struck his gavel and my uncle was gone for a year and a half. True to his nature, he led men even in prison—Bible studies, a veterans' group, teaching some of the illiterate how to read using Goosebumps books. Every day after his five hundred pushups, he tackled science-fiction novels—Philip K. Dick, Ursula K. Le Guin, Samuel R. Delany. He even tried writing some of his own, though he never shared the pages with me because he thought they were "straight-up baby shit, like the kind from a green alien infant." And it wasn't all smooth sailing for my uncle. He said there were nights, moonless nights he thought of nothing but hanging himself with his bedsheets. He thought about what he'd done to the old woman, the sudden yet prolonged obliteration to her family. He thought about her husband, about exchanging letters with him, gaining a pen pal, but deciding against it in the end.

Then he was released. He was different, calmer somehow, and more importantly, no longer in possession of a spotless record. Nobody would know that far away, eight people in a village survived because of him. Not to mention myself, his nephew he'd adopted after getting back from overseas, himself barely old enough to qualify as a grown man. Taking care of his dead sister's son on a promise. Now it'd be a miracle, he said without saying it, if the McDonald's empire would call him back, make room for him in their legion. Flip frozen meat. Prepare Happy Meals for spoiled brats.

"You know, chump," he says. "You can do things proper, by the book and shit, but all it takes is one bad day. And that's all anyone'll remember. Ain't a damn thing you can do to change it."

He rubs the tattoo on his arm—*Grace and Hope* inked in black Olde English font—drops his head.

"I didn't drink before the military," he mutters. "Not a single Goddamn drop."

He glances at me, smiles weakly, still rubbing his arm as if it were sore, fresh. Then he lowers his head again, does something I haven't seen since the day he was locked up.

I hold him, let him weep on my shoulder.

Troop's beside us nudging our legs.

"Ay there," Uncle Juan says to him. "It's all good, boy, everything's good."

Before my mom died, Uncle Juan gave her his word that he'd watch after me. His bond unbroken of as yet—each day that responsibility shifting like the gears of an old clock.

Mom had this saying, the only one I recollect: *When things get heavy, play a song and take it steady.*

"Get a room, you two," I say to Uncle Juan, Troop tongue-attacking his face.

In my closet I flick on the light, pull out from a cardboard box a portable record player Mom had bought at a garage sale. Then from a plastic bag I take out a dozen old vinyls, thumb through them until I find the one.

Back in the living room it hits me: the closet light hadn't bothered me a damn bit.

I plug in the record player, carefully remove the Sam & Dave record from its vintage tattered cover. It's either exceptionally valuable, or near worthless.

Our jumbo golden retriever's on Uncle Juan's lap, looking pleased as a fat cat.

"Gonna play some jams, huh?"

"No," I answer sarcastically, gently setting the needle down.

A scratch, an electric guitar riff, blaring brass horns. Then, as if from the clouds, the legendary duo known as Sam & Dave, all the way from Memphis, Tennessee.

Comin' to you on a dusty road
Good lovin' I got a truck load
And when you get it you got something
So don't worry cause I'm coming

"Damn, son, haven't heard this joint in a minute! Your momma's favorite."

I snap open the curtains and sunlight bum-rushes our apartment, my body. From our view on the third floor, the city's as inviting as a pair of wide-open legs. No, safer than that, more cliché. Let's rewind: From our view on the third floor, the city's as inviting, as proud and beguiling as a wide-open story. Timeworn, massive, an unfinished masterpiece.

I press my ear against the warm window glass, listen—the vibrations of sound and movement. I hear my name forming on someone's lips. You rang, m'Lord? Dogs barking, cars honking, kids shouting. A girl hopscotching a rainbow-chalked sidewalk. A motorcycle cop lurking around the street corner; someone with a baggy red tee flicking him off. Two blocks past, at the 7-Eleven, I know the Doomsday Curb Preacher is there with his eye patch, demanding passersby to repent for their sins. I see ballers at Hooper Park breaking ankles, talking hella trash, the pimp in a giant suit who dubs himself Purple Rain, a new plus-sized lady by his side. Inside one of the distant skyscrapers, a boardroom shyster—the Devil himself. Everyone down there playing their roles, hoping to catch a break. The seven angels who'll soon swoop down, trumpets in hand, crying in celebration. You're alive, and you are free. You are free. Free.

I turn around—Uncle Juan blank-staring, Troop panting to the rhythm of the scratchy record.

"The hell's gotten in you, chump?"

I tap the windowpane, point to the meridian, to somewhere in the backdrop. I say:

"Brand-new day. Word?"

Uncle Juan rubs his tattoo once more, then he stands, walks over, peers outside. He sees what I see because there's brand-new light in his eyes, his watery eyes shining like polished pennies, like an elusive clean slate. He claps my shoulder and repeats:

"Word."

Killer Leanings

∞

I'm driven to Death in strange ways.

Oh, I limit my drinks; I count calories; I exercise daily; I smoke only on the Fourth of July; I believe in Heaven; I help a brother when he's down. But I also walk against traffic; I don't wear my seatbelt; I've stood outside in thunderstorms; I hold packages close to my chest, cut the tape in the direction of my heart; I press my weight against upper-story railings.

It's a statistical anomaly, a miracle, that I'm here. That any of us are. We fight against it daily, wanting—always—to be somewhere else.

Bread and Bologna

∞

The last time I saw her as she was—not the very last time, for that would come later, when her mind had long abandoned her—she fixed me a bologna sandwich, nothing else inside.

The bread and meat were fresh, and she so thin I wondered when she'd last fed herself.

When Grandpa was still alive—this was well after his final sortie in the Cessna, whose scraps I dream are strewn from Mexico to Mount Rushmore in the shape of Our Lady of Guadalupe—we used to say his stomach—his pansa—resembled a gigantic elephant's. Our family was the kind to deploy redundant adjectives.

"This is delicious," I said one bite in, a small white lie.

"Did I ever tell you about my father, a brilliant businessman and orator?" my grandmother asked.

"Not really," I answered, a huge white lie.

"He'd do people's taxes for free. He taught them how to speak English. He was a good, smart man. All the brains you have, you get it from my side.

"Don't you ever forget it," my grandmother said, before ten minutes passed and she asked me again about her father, the man to whom I owe my intelligence.

The patience I retain in memory recall, in writing poetry—for I squandered my late-twenties studying for an English literature degree—I severely lack in real life.

A little girl once approached me in a café and asked what I was reading. I looked up, spotted her beautiful mother smiling at me, and with a shaky knee I answered the child, "Just a tiny book."

Some days—especially under bright, clear skies—I find the sound of acoustic guitar emotionally exhausting. Not detestable but draining. I can't say how. I don't know why.

"It's like my life happens only to become somebody else's story," my best friend from high school had said, months before he enlisted in the Marines and got blown up in Afghanistan.

"Yep," was all I could muster in reply.

It's sad, this whole enterprise. Maddening. But also, quite often, drop-dead gorgeous.

Face it. Fucking admit it.

There's no story here. Eighteen months as of this scribbling embroiled in a global pandemic—there's no story here.

What I feel, I feel mostly for myself. What I write, I write mostly for myself, so that death may compress me into a flashing thought, a stranger's briefest interest.

My name, my words, learn and understand them—or I am a war machine trapped in this period condensed by the laws of physics, the logic of grammar. And this one.

Kiss them. Release me.

If I could go back, I'd lie to my grandmother so much better. Instead of "delicious," I'd call her last bologna sandwich "scrumptious." "The best sandwich ever." Something ridiculous. Then I'd pick up all the crumpled tissues of Kleenex she'd tossed behind her sofa, along with her wedding band. And gently place the ring back on her slender finger.

"Did I ever tell you about my father?" she would ask.

"Not really," I would lie.

But this exercise, we know, is tampering with evidence. Disrespectful. And I like to believe I behave respectfully toward the dead.

Author's Note

To Professor Ito Romo, for opening the floodgates, for pushing me to write clearer and to abandon ship when stories burned. To Jennifer Lloyd, for always lending me your ear, for nourishing support and love. To my siblings (in chronological order): Sonny, Andy, Mike, Melissa, Aaron. Because life would be worse without y'all. To Will Pate, my laconic publisher cooler than cool. To Marcus Salinas, for the greatest gift: laughter. To Will Rodriguez, for "published author" vibes. To Karl Switzer, for seeing in me all that you do (since eighth grade). To Mom and Pops, for everything.

Acknowledgements

101 Words: "Burning of Non La," "Killer Leanings," "Rainbow Suspenders"

365tomorrows: "In Space, Your Meals Are Determined by Hired Cooks"

Ariel Chart: "Places"

Defenestration: "Long Time No See"

Every Day Fiction: "Family Feud," "Happy Enough," "Milkshake," "Should've Just Stuck With the Damn Doritos"

The Fusty Nut Review: "Discretion," "If I Drown, Play Some Bill Withers for Me," "Rice Krispies Treat Conundrum"

Me First Magazine: "Pancakes and Waffles"

Mystery Tribune: "An Exercise in Futility," "Angels and Elves," "Blind," "Chicken Run," "City Lights From the Upside Down," "Gun, With Zero Music," "Kolson," "Pepperoni," "The Post-it Manifesto," "The Yellow Slide"

The Piker Press: "Even-Steven"

Points in Case: "The Sad Tale of the Inflatable Wacky Tube Man"

Red Fez: "Chipped," "The Wrestler"

The Rye Whiskey Review: "Plenty of Time"

San Antonio Review: "All the Pretty Paintings," "Men Without Hearts, Inc.," "Santa Always Blows His Cover"

Schlock! Webzine: "Coke Machine," "The Consideration," "Kodak Moment"

Yes, Poetry: "The Savage Screwball"

About the Author

Alex Z. Salinas is the author of two full-length poetry collections from Hekate Publishing: *WARBLES*, and *DREAMT, or The Lingering Phantoms of Equinox*. He holds an M.A. in English Literature and Language from St. Mary's University. He lives in San Antonio, Texas.

Other Books by Alex Z. Salinas

WARBLES

DREAMT, or The Lingering Phantoms of Equinox

About SAR Press

City Lights From the Upside Down is the second non-journal book-length publication of *San Antonio Review*'s book publishing imprint, SAR Press.

SAR Press, an imprint of *San Antonio Review*, an international literary, arts and ideas journal since 2017, is devoted to publishing book-length works by interesting voices.

Learn more at sareview.org/sar-press.

San Antonio Review publishes original essays, poetry, art, reviews, theory and other work twice a week on its website. Print issues are published at the publisher's discretion. Founded in San Antonio in 2017, *SAR* is based in Austin, Texas.

San Antonio Review is devoted to serving as a gathering space outside academia, the market and government for writers, artists, scholars, activists, workers, students, parents and others to express their perspectives and reflections on our shared world and help develop visions of our collective future. Funded by its publisher's income from his day jobs, donations and the sale of print editions and other materials and led and maintained by an all-volunteer editorial collective, *SAR* is not beholden to any institution, organization or ideology.

SAR is a seed.[1] Planted and tended, we hope it grows. We can at best provide a hospitable environment and some nurturing care to the pieces we publish and ensure their dissemination and preservation in hopes some future finder may be spurred to positive action by what they share. The *SAR* Editorial Collective is an experiment[2] in the prefigurative politics of constructive, everyday resistance.[3] That is, *SAR* is trying to create a publishing organization today that reflects the world as it might be; that proves an alternative is possible and things may be otherwise.

Learn more at sareview.org

Also available from SAR Press:

Mel Bay's Book of the Dead by Harold Whit Williams.

Also available from *San Antonio Review*:

San Antonio Review

Always read free at sareview.org

1. Initial credit for likening *SAR* to a tree goes to our inaugural poetry editor Alex Z. Salinas in his introduction to our second print issue.
2. Süß, Rahel. "Horizontal Experimentalism: Rethinking Democratic Resistance." *Philosophy & Social Criticism*, Aug. 2021, https://doi.org/10.1177/01914537211033016.
3. Kristin Wiksell (2020) Worker cooperatives for social change: knowledge-making through constructive resistance within the capitalist market economy, *Journal of Political Power*, 13:2, 201-216, DOI: 10.1080/2158379X.2020.1764803

CPSIA information can be obtained
at www.ICGtesting.com
Printed in the USA
LVHW031756181021
700772LV00014B/723